"I appreciate your motives, Ms. Stewart.

"But you must understand, I can't allow my employees to make a practice of telling their relatives I've married them."

Here it came. Damon was firing her, after all.

Just then, Mercy heard a noise and glanced beyond the glass door. "Oh, no," she moaned, jumping up. "It's Grandpa. What shall we do?"

"How long have we been married?"

She shrugged. "A couple of weeks."

Surprising her, he took her hand and pulled her into his lap. "Then we'd be on our honeymoon."

She fell onto his lap, able to do nothing more than stare at him.

"Which would you prefer," he asked, "that I kiss you, or just gaze lovingly into your eyes?"

Dear Reader,

I married for math. I was so lousy at the subject, I was terrified at the idea of ever having to help my children struggle with arithmetic homework. While dating, I secretly schemed to catch a guy who didn't blink an eye when asked the square root of any number. I also wanted a guy who liked kids, was tall, witty and handsome. Too much to ask, you say? Well, what's life worth, if we don't *dare to dream!*

I've been married for some years now to a tall, witty, handsome man. At the age of fourteen, my youngest son—upon hearing the shocking news that I had no idea how to find the square root of *anything*—created a computer program that would give the information whenever I might need it. Considering my lack of computer talent, I hugged him and said, "Honey, if I need to know the square root of anything, I'll just give you a call—or your brother or your daddy." Even though I've never needed square root help, I know my family's here to support me if necessary. Maybe I sound flippant, but really I'm not. A loving family is a blessing, and I honestly wish you that blessing. Also, I hope you'll enjoy Damon and Mercy's romance—and the family ties that trap them into a make-believe marriage. Okay, okay, I'll give you a hint, the secret has nothing to do with math!

Sincerely,

Renee Roszel

MAKE-BELIEVE MARRIAGE
Renee Roszel

Harlequin Books

TORONTO • NEW YORK • LONDON
AMSTERDAM • PARIS • SYDNEY • HAMBURG
STOCKHOLM • ATHENS • TOKYO • MILAN
MADRID • WARSAW • BUDAPEST • AUCKLAND

If you purchased this book without a cover you should be aware
that this book is stolen property. It was reported as "unsold and
destroyed" to the publisher, and neither the author nor the
publisher has received any payment for this "stripped book."

To Norda Roszel Lyles
One of the sweetest people in the world—
and you're *my* sister!
Love, Renee

ISBN 0-373-03370-2

MAKE-BELIEVE MARRIAGE

Copyright © 1995 by Renee Roszel Wilson.

First North American Publication 1995.

All rights reserved. Except for use in any review, the reproduction or
utilization of this work in whole or in part in any form by any electronic,
mechanical or other means, now known or hereafter invented, including
xerography, photocopying and recording, or in any information storage
or retrieval system, is forbidden without the written permission of the
publisher, Harlequin Enterprises Limited, 225 Duncan Mill Road,
Don Mills, Ontario, Canada M3B 3K9.

All characters in this book have no existence outside the imagination of
the author and have no relation whatsoever to anyone bearing the same
name or names. They are not even distantly inspired by any individual
known or unknown to the author, and all incidents are pure invention.

This edition published by arrangement with Harlequin Enterprises B.V.

® and TM are trademarks of the publisher. Trademarks indicated with
® are registered in the United States Patent and Trademark Office, the
Canadian Trade Marks Office and in other countries.

Printed in U.S.A.

CHAPTER ONE

"DARLING, DAMON," Josephine DeMorney gushed, patting her grandnephew's hand. "Here comes the angel I've been telling you about." From her usual place at the far end of the yacht's ten-foot dining table, the elderly woman, clad in green sweats and a yellow feather boa, beckoned with a bejeweled hand toward Mercy. "Come here, my dear."

Mercy's stride faltered as she entered the dining salon, and she prayed her misstep had gone unnoticed. The second occupant at the table could have been none other than the great and powerful wizard of the Panther Automotive Corporation, Damon DeMorney. The newspaper photos she'd seen of him didn't do the man justice.

The complete opposite of his flighty great-aunt, he was clad in clothes that were sedate yet in vogue. His lightweight cashmere jacket was an icy blue, fitting precisely across stunningly wide shoulders. His cotton shirt was of the ultra-expensive Italian variety, and his abstract-print tie no doubt cost more than the entire complement of the yacht crew's uniforms.

Since the dining table was topped by a rare piece of etched glass, she could see that his long legs were

stretched nearly the width of the table. He wore gray
slacks and matching wing tips. Entirely, utterly elegant.

He glanced her way at his aunt's prodding. His strong
features closed a bit, going from amusement at one of
Jo's offbeat quips to mildly curious. His eyes, a deep,
rich green, narrowed, but his dashing smile didn't waver.

Mercy just stared. That grin dimpled his cheeks. It was
an intriguing, crooked grin, masculine—gorgeous in
newspaper photos, but almost frighteningly so in person. It occurred to her that she'd never seen eyes so
vividly green as his, or lashes quite so long—tipped with
silver. Oh, and that neatly trimmed mane of hair! She'd
known he was blond from his photographs, but now, in
his presence, his hair glistened like white gold. Platinum, she supposed was the word for it.

*How could she ever have bragged to her poor, sickly
grandfather that this paragon of male beauty was her
husband! She should have her tongue ripped out for such
a brash lie! They weren't in the same universe, let alone
the same league—matrimonially speaking! He'd probably marry some countess or movie star. Not an untidy
cook, for heaven's sake.*

"There's my little kitchen saint." Josephine smiled,
patting the general vicinity of the curls of one of her nu-
merous wigs. This model, Mercy liked to think of as the
"Cher." Totally unfit for a woman of seventy, it was a
frightful riot of brown ringlets that stood out in frothy
chaos around her unlined, plump face. Still, she carried
off her bizarre dress code with the sweet aplomb of those
who don't concern themselves with the small-minded of
the world. Aunt Jo, as she liked to be called, loved life,

loved her grandnephew, herself, everybody else, and her two potbellied pigs—not necessarily in that order. "Why, Damon," she exuded, "on Mercy's diet, in just four weeks my womanly hormones have shot up to lethal levels." She winked. "I'm a deadly catch now. You just wait and see."

Damon's grin grew wry as he eyed the mandarin salads on the luncheon tray Mercy was carrying. "Am I to assume that by the end of this cruise I'll be singing soprano?"

He was looking directly at her now, and she found herself tongue-tied. Though she knew his remark had been joking, she couldn't seem to get her lips to form a grin. All she could manage was a wide-eyed stare as his glance raked her slender form, from her white deck shoes upward to the tailored, thigh-length shorts and on past her knit shirt to the fresh blush on her cheeks.

"Silly, silly, boy," Jo admonished, filling the breach with a healthy titter. "A little soya flower and red clover sprouts would never stand a chance against the raging masculinity of your hormones."

Mercy felt an awkward thrill at the mention of his masculinity. She had to agree with Aunt Jo. Damon DeMorney didn't appear to be in imminent danger of losing much ground in *that* area merely by eating a little "pasture food."

She managed to clear her throat, and belatedly offered, "I—I'll prepare whatever type of dishes you want, sir. I can do steak and potatoes, too."

A well-shaped brow rose as he took in that information. "I'm gratified to hear that." He turned toward his aunt, apparently dismissing her from his mind. She felt the vaguest sense of having been chastised, as though it should go without saying that the DeMorneys would never hire a chef who couldn't do anything asked of her. Or should she feel complimented that he naturally assumed she was completely capable? The man's ambiguous manner was probably one reason he was so successful. He had a gift for keeping rivals off-balance.

Aunt Jo waved airily toward Mercy. "Come over here, dear. Meet my contrary grandnephew." She grazed his square jaw with her fingers. "I simply couldn't let him leave on his little cruise without seeing him for a few fleeting minutes. If I didn't have that important bingo tournament, I'd stay on board and go with you." She sighed with all the theatrics of a dying Camille. "Damon so rarely visits me, I can hardly recall his face."

How could anyone forget that face! Mercy's mind cried—those firm, sensual lips, that stubborn jaw, and the almost supernatural beauty of those silvery lashes and that sexy-angel hair. She chewed the inside of her cheek, hoping her expression betrayed nothing of her wayward thoughts.

Damon was grinning at his great-aunt. "You fraud. Do you really think I'd believe you'd rather have a lapdog than an income?"

Aunt Jo threw back her head and guffawed, both pudgy hands going up to hold her heavy wig in place. "Touché," she chortled. "But I must say, I wonder how you can really be running the company when all I ever see of you is that rakish face in the Miami papers with yet another society nymphet." She shook a beringed finger at him. "And there's the core of the very predicament I must discuss with you, my dear. Your reputation as a playboy and your tyrannical ways with your board of directors is becoming a sticky issue I think you must address."

Mercy couldn't see Damon's face, but had a feeling he'd stopped smiling. Josephine beckoned to Mercy again. "Come here, dear, you be the impartial judge."

Mercy hesitated. She knew Josephine got quirky ideas into her head, and she had a feeling this wasn't one of her best. "I—I..."

She had no chance to complete her thought for Damon shifted to face her, his jaw working. It was clear he didn't have any intention of his yacht's chef sitting in judgment of him. With a thinly polite smile, he said, "Just leave the lunches, Miss..."

She swallowed. "Stewart. Ms. Mercy Stewart."

He nodded dismissively. "*Ms.* Stewart. I'm sure you have duties to attend to."

A pig grunted loudly from his sprawled position between Aunt Jo and Damon. Reaching down to pat it, Aunt Jo huffed, "Desi, you're so right. If that's to be Damon's attitude, I don't know what I can do for him." Directing herself back to her grandnephew, she scolded, "You realize, of course, that Clayton Stringman has most of your cousins quite charmed. Even though you own forty-one percent of the company stock, I'm beginning to worry about your ability to hold on to control—even with my five percent solidly behind you. You are aware that Clayton and his father before him have been loyal company men, and to be utterly frank, the board is simply frightened of you. *Yes,*" she admonished with a nod so strong her wig skewed down over her eyes. Righting it, she added, "I repeat—*frightened.* They feel you've bullied them into over—er—exercising in—in a poor envelope—''

Damon frowned at his aunt. "I can see Clayton has been lecturing you, too. But I believe you mean, overextending in a poor economy. And that aggressive tactic," he counseled softly, "along with an excellent product line, is exactly what has made us the success we are."

Jo shrugged. "Well, Clayton is loudly touting the need for caution. That appeals to the board right now. If I were you, I'd not take my warning lightly. I know, Damon, dear, you've rarely sought or accepted advice, and you're a loner due to your family's dreadful..." She faltered, looked pained, then regained her poise. "Well, anyway, just listen to me when I say, *at least* promise that you'll look into more conservative strategies. And for heaven's sake, get that handsome face of yours out of the gossip columns. If you don't expend more energy charming the board and less charming the ladies, for the first time in the company's history, someone outside the family will be elected Chief Executive Officer."

Mercy was placing the salads and Josephine's pot of ginseng coffee substitute on the table as swiftly as possible. She knew this conversation was none of her business, and she shouldn't be a party to it. From the look on Damon's face, it was clear that he was working hard to keep his anger under control.

She forced her eyes down and purposefully closed her features. But this new development was intriguing. Could Damon DeMorney be on the verge of toppling from his majestic seat at the head of Panther Automotive? Well, if *her* plan succeeded, she just might help topple him!

When she straightened, preparing to go, Damon's gaze snagged hers, and she was struck by the impact. His eyes were dazzling in his irritation, like fire-lit emeralds. Managing a weak, employee smile, she murmured, "Will there be anything else?" She breathed a sigh of relief that her voice sounded so placid. She was certainly not placid. She was staring into Damon DeMorney's sparkling gaze, wishing his *opponent* all the luck in the world. As far as she was concerned, the DeMorneys were where they were because they'd crawled over the backs of innocents. Maybe it was time they took a hard fall from grace and somebody outside the family grabbed the reins of the company. She was all for that!

"Nothing else, right now," he told her coolly. When she'd turned to go, he added, "And nothing further from you, either, Aunt Jo. You know under my management the company has had a major profit increase every year for the past five years. Stringman's chief talent is his knack for exploiting situations. He's a slimy little yes-man, and if he gets board approval, I swear he'll bring this company to its knees in two years—"

"Oh, that reminds me," Jo interrupted in an airy trill. "Mercy, dear, you neglected to tell us what you've prepared for the rest of our meal."

She was taken aback. Jo didn't seem to register that she'd just been soundly reprimanded by her grand-nephew and that food had nothing at all to do with the subject they'd been discussing.

Wishing she could escape to calm down and absorb what she'd learned, she slowly turned back. She tried to address Aunt Jo, the DeMorney who'd hired her, yet her gaze drifted awkwardly toward Damon. His mouth was set in a firm line, his nostrils flaring with outrage. He obviously didn't care a twit about what they were having for lunch. Taking a calming breath, she began, "Steamed clams with a buttery flour roux, seasoned with chopped parsley, green onions and fresh herbs..."

She went on to describe the meal by rote, anxious to get away. This was the most tedious part of her job, but Aunt Jo relished the telling. Unfortunately, Mercy was having a hard time keeping her mind on the menu. Her glance was drawn again to Damon's platinum mane of hair. It looked thick, yet fine. She imagined it would be wonderful beneath her fingers—to stroke and pat.

"We're having *hair* for dessert?" Jo cried, horrified.

The aghast tone drew Mercy back to what she was supposed to be doing. "I beg your pardon?" she asked, not sure she'd heard right.

Damon sat back, his expression skeptical. "My aunt doesn't seem to be thrilled with the idea of eating hair for dessert." His eyes had lost some of their angry glitter, and Mercy had a vague fear that he was amused by her slip of the tongue. She had an awful feeling he'd had people surreptitiously admire his pale metallic hair before—never making quite the fool of themselves as she had, however.

Clearing her throat and feeling irritation at herself for her slip, she backpedaled. "I—er—said—Rasp-beeeeerr-y—Raspberry yogurt tarts. You must have misunderstood me." It was a transparent lie, but her pride forced her to try it.

"Ah," Damon murmured with a slow nod. "I'm sure that was it."

Mercy faced him, cringing inwardly. His eyes had narrowed further, and he didn't appear all that amused any longer. He wasn't buying it, and obviously didn't appreciate her weak fib. He had some nerve to disapprove of lies, considering his father's, and probably *his,* business practices! With great effort, she kept her dark thoughts to herself and dragged her eyes from his.

It upset her to realize her hands were shaking and she clutched them together. She lied badly—even small, unimportant ones. This man could read people, see through lies. He was not one to be trifled with, and Mercy had a sneaking dread that trying to put anything over on him would be very dangerous, if not impossible.

"Oh, good!" Jo exclaimed. "Raspberry yogurt tarts are a favorite of Lucy's." Reaching down, she caressed the squashed-in snout of her female pig, lounging on her other side. "I do hope you've made extra."

Mercy nodded, backing away. Though she was ignoring Damon with all her might, she knew his gaze was riveted on her, taking in her humiliation. "There are plenty of tarts," she mumbled.

Forcing herself to meet Damon's gaze once again, she asked, "Would you like coffee now, or with dessert?"

"Now." He crossed his arms over his chest, adding softly, "Sugar."

She hesitated. He'd called her *sugar!* She felt an upwelling of indignation. "Excuse me, Mr. DeMorney," she objected, "but I must insist you call me Ms. Stewart."

He'd turned away, but when she made her staunch, if a bit tremulous demand, he shifted back. This time his eyes grew openly amused, and his mouth quirked to display a flash of teeth. "Forgive me for offending your sense of propriety, *Ms.* Stewart. However, I meant, I take sugar in my coffee."

She colored fiercely. Wishing she were dead, she could only manage a stiff nod before pivoting away. He'd merely anticipated her next question when he'd said "sugar," she'd taken it wrong. She wondered what demented quirk of her mind had made her do that. Now he probably believed she thought he was irresistible or something. Well, he couldn't be more wrong!

Without paying much attention to her surroundings, she hurried through the luxurious dining area and connecting salon. Always before, she'd enjoyed gazing around that bright, open space, alive with indirect lighting and pale tones. Deep-pile, beige carpeting ran the fifty-foot length of the dining and salon area. Maple and ash wood had been washed by a white stain to emphasize the grain. Touches of lively cinnamons, greens and vermilions from artwork and sculptures warmed and humanized the room. She loved the room—usually—but right now she saw none of its beauty. All she could see was Damon DeMorney's taunting grin. *Oh, what an idiot she'd made of herself!*

THE YACHT'S SPARKLING and spacious galley was tucked into the port side of the main deck. Glancing absently out the window over the sink, she noticed clouds rolling in. Too bad. The weather had been so nice for the past month. She wondered if the rain clouds were a foreboding of bad things to come. No, *no*—that was just her guilt getting to her again. She mustn't dwell on it.

Stirring the clam sauce, she nervously peered at her watch, deciding she had a few more minutes before Aunt Jo rang for the main course. She'd been the yacht's chef for over a month, and she hadn't been found out, yet. But the thought of trying to deceive a man as perceptive as Mr. DeMorney made her go weak in the knees.

No matter how impossible the obstacles seemed, she was determined to clear her grandfather's name before he died. The sweet man had lived too many years with a cloud over his reputation. Unfortunately she was no closer to her objective than she had been four weeks ago when she'd started working for Josephine. And things weren't looking a bit better for her now that her "bride-groom" had entered the picture.

She'd never done anything even mildly underhanded before, and she didn't know if she could continue to get away with her wild fabrication—having to look into Damon DeMorney's shrewd eyes day after day....

She shook off the foolish thought. He might be what the news magazines called "a genius in the automotive industry," but he was no mind reader. If she was careful, he couldn't possibly find her out before she sprang her trap. She just had to bide her time, pretend to have nothing more on her mind than her cooking, and continue to force herself to act like a compliant employee.

Poor Grandpa Goodeve was in such fragile health. His doctor had warned her that he probably had only months left to live. Mercy had decided that just in case she couldn't find out the truth in time, she could at least make his final days happy. So she'd called him with the Big Lie—that as the *Silver Cat*'s chef, she'd met and married Damon DeMorney. What harm, she'd reasoned, could a few cheering phone calls do?

When her butter roux sauce began to thicken, she took it off the flame and eyed her watch again. This delicate sauce was like a hothouse flower. It didn't languish well. She hoped Aunt Jo would ring soon.

Rather than torture herself with wild fantasies of discovery, Mercy decided she'd be better off thinking positively. She still marveled at her good luck. Twenty-two years old and just out of the Culinary Institute of America, she hadn't been the most experienced applicant Josephine had interviewed. Shaking her head, she once again thanked providence for her good fortune. It seemed the older woman had so many health concerns, she'd had a hard time finding a chef who could keep up with them. However, since healthy eating was one of Mercy's top priorities, she'd found favor with Aunt Jo right away.

She'd taken the job thinking of all the DeMorneys as grasping, greedy snobs, but she'd grown to like Aunt Jo and felt bad about her deception. She didn't think Josephine DeMorney had been a party to the conspiracy to frame her grandfather and hated the thought of hurting her.

But that might be a moot point now. She'd been stuck on the yacht all month, nowhere near any files where she might get the answers to how her grandfather had been framed and financially ruined.

As she arranged food on the luncheon plates, she thought again of how poor, sweet Otis had never even defended himself when Kennard made his accusations of mismanagement. The harsher term Kennard used had been "embezzlement." He'd offered to buy Otis's half of the company stock for a fair but bargain price, and in return he wouldn't press charges.

Otis had been the automotive designer, a sensitive artist, not a hard-nosed businessman like Kennard DeMorney. He'd merely assumed he'd done something stupid and accepted his firing, sold his stock for Kennard's price—stock that today was worth many millions of dollars.

It had been Otis's daughter, Mercy's mother, who'd complained to Mercy year after year that she was sure Otis had been framed by Kennard DeMorney, conniving to get the whole company for himself.

After all this time, Mercy's mother was dead and gone, and Otis was dying. If her grandfather's reputation were to be cleansed, it had to be now—had to be by Mercy—so he could know it before he died. She only hoped that after this cruise to the Caymans, she'd have a chance to work in the Miami mansion and get access to some old company books she'd heard were stored in the basement.

The green call light flashed on, startling Mercy. She untied her apron and put it aside, then picked up the silver tray. Having a thought, she set it back down to scan herself in the stainless-steel refrigerator door. She grimaced, grateful she'd checked. Taking a damp kitchen towel, she swiped at a brown splotch on her breast pocket where the ship's name was embroidered with silver thread. When it didn't leave a stain she breathed a sigh of relief.

Tucking a stray strand of light brown hair back into the French twist at her nape, she shook her head at her murky reflection. At moments like this she wished she were just a tad neater at her job. But neat or not, she was a good chef. That's what counted. Aunt Jo had rarely ventured into the galley, anyway. And Mercy always left the place spotless when the day's work was done. So what was the harm of a little clutter?

Sucking in an apprehensive breath, she retrieved the tray and headed abaft along the narrow hall toward the dining salon. She was startled to see Lucy, Aunt Jo's female potbellied pig, shuffling her way. She grinned wanly at the odd-looking but sweet-natured pet. "He makes you nervous, too, huh?" she whispered.

When Lucy snorted in seeming response, Mercy couldn't suppress a melancholy chuckle.

THEY'D HEADED OUT to sea an hour ago, and the ocean was getting rougher and rougher. Mercy swallowed, feeling a tinge of seasickness, and prayed it would quickly pass. She'd rarely been seasick, but the waters had always been calm until now. Or maybe it was just knowing that the crafty Mr. DeMorney was so near that was making her feel sick. As she wiped the countertops, she tried desperately to get her mind off her queasy stomach and on tonight's menu.

What would a fire-eating tyrant eat? Raw meat? Nails? After a month of preparing dishes of bean sprouts and tofu, she was going to have to shift gears quickly. *Ah*, she thought perversely, *maybe, for dessert tonight, he'd like an arsenic apple pie!*

"Ms. Stewart?" came a deep voice from the vicinity of the galley entrance.

Mercy jerked about, startled that a fire-eating tyrant could move so silently. "Yes—yes, sir?" Heat rushed up

her cheeks at her recent wayward thoughts and she hoped
once again that his keen gaze couldn't penetrate her
brain.

He was lounging against the doorjamb and had
changed into blue chambray boxer shorts that displayed
his long legs to perfection. His washed-cotton shirt
matched exactly. Except for the color, he looked surprisingly like one of the crew. Quite diplomatic of him,
Mercy mused caustically. A tiny, inner voice said, *Nice
legs, too—tanned, muscular....* She worked at ignoring
the voice. Damon DeMorney's legs were none of her
business—no matter what she'd told her grandfather
about being his blushing bride.

"What the hell happened in here?" he asked, his gaze
critical as it shifted about the room.

She fought down a surge of nausea, and clung to the
locker handle. She was going to be sick, and his accusing tone wasn't doing her stomach any good. "I—I was
just getting a mop," she mumbled, feeling dizzy.

"That's very optimistic. Personally, I'd opt for a bull-
dozer." His glance fell to a brown puddle of sauce that
had dribbled from the countertop to the floor. "Ms.
Stewart," he admonished, "with the seas this rough, you
could slip on that muck and kill yourself. I've got enough
on my mind. I don't need—" He bit off his remark,
seeming preoccupied. Maybe he was more disturbed
about this Clayton Stringman problem than he'd let on
to Josephine. "Never mind," he said less harshly. "I just
came in for some coffee." He walked to the coffee-
maker, got down a mug and poured himself some.

"You could call for coffee, sir."

"I was passing by." He added a teaspoon of sugar, turned to go, then faced her again. "I won't tell you your job, Ms. Stewart. I'm sure you're very good or my aunt wouldn't have hired you." He indicated the galley. "But try not to kill yourself or anyone else."

She nodded, swallowing hard. Her seasickness was getting worse by the second.

He peered closely at her. "Do you feel all right?"

"The seas are—uh—a little rough," she offered honestly.

"You should take something."

She blinked. Had she detected a hint of actual humanity in his tone? Surely not! Avoiding the urge to clutch her cramping stomach, she managed, "Yes, sir." She squared her shoulders with effort. "And don't worry. The galley will be shipshape in an hour."

He raised a brow, as though dubious that such a feat were possible even if she'd felt perfect.

"Feel free to come back and check," she blurted, his doubtful silence pricking her pride.

For a moment he studied her with watchful eyes. She had a feeling he was trying to reach into her mind. Offering him a fake smile, she hoped it would throw him off the scent. She knew her tone had been snappish, and he no doubt wondered why. She certainly didn't want him to discover her true feelings for him or the real reason she was working here. After a few seconds he shrugged dismissively, probably deciding her shortness had been because she didn't feel well. "All right, Ms. Stewart, since you insist, I'll see you in an hour." As suddenly and silently as he had appeared, he was gone.

Mercy's stomach lurched, and she gave the empty door a sour look. She had an urge to call after him and tell him she had *not* insisted, and if she never saw him again it would be fine with her! But she was afraid to open her mouth. She only longed to be alive an hour.

CHAPTER TWO

DRAMAMINE gave Mercy violent hiccups, and seasick patches blurred her vision so badly she could hardly see. So, not long ago she'd resorted to borrowing some prescription seasick medication from Malcolm, one of the ship's stewards. The pill had been like a miracle drug, and Mercy was no longer hiccuping or seeing double. She was, however, feeling a little odd.

She checked her watch. It was past time for Mr. I'll-Take-That-Dare to come back and inspect her galley, which was now as spotless as she'd promised it would be. Well, she simply couldn't wait around for him any longer. It was time for the captain's mint tea.

She headed out of the galley, gripping the handrail, working to shake off a sudden fuzzy-headedness. The sea was rough, and she almost missed a step. Luckily, she managed not to spill a drop of tea. She giggled, then sobered. What was funny about that?

Mounting the top step to the pilothouse, she was appalled to see Mr. DeMorney standing beside the yacht's portly captain, Pitt Meyers. Captain Meyers was forever on a diet, and constantly hungry. So, Mercy brought him his daily sugar high—a glass of mint tea with three spoonfuls of sugar. She knew it wasn't good for him, but it kept him from downing an entire box of Oreos, his usual afternoon snack. It seemed the lesser of two evils.

"Ah, my tea," Pitt bellowed, his jowly face brightening when he saw Mercy's stiff-backed approach.

She couldn't understand why it looked like such a long distance from the stairs to the control panel where the two men stood. The last time she'd been up there it had only been a few feet away.

With measured steps, she inched her way toward them. Gone was the rich, hand-rubbed wood paneling Mercy remembered. She found herself moving through what seemed to be a long, narrow shaft. Blinking several times, she tried to regain her perspective. What in heaven's name was wrong?

Damon was watching her closely, as though he thought she'd grown an extra head. She heard a giggle and frowned. Neither Captain Meyers nor Mr. DeMorney appeared to be likely candidates for a fit of giggles. She peered at them both. Neither was even smiling now.

When she finally made the ghastly length of the pilothouse and handed Captain Meyers his tea, she breathed a sigh. What a chore that had been. With a tentative nod toward her nemesis, Mr. DeMorney, she said, "If I'd known you were going to be here, sir, I'd have brought you some, too, *tea*."

He assessed her with a curious frown. "Are you all right, Miss Stewart?"

She took a deep breath, determined not to allow this insufferable, self-important playboy to intimidate her. "If you'll notice, Mr. De-Moralize..." She poked him in the chest, noting a peculiar expression flash across his face. "I am no longer a messy galley! So there!" She took a step back, but the rolling sea caused her to lurch sideways, barely missing the captain's drinking arm. "Oops," Mercy murmured, shaking her head. "That was a close one, Skipper." She couldn't control a peal of laughter, and for the life of her, she couldn't figure out why. "Mustn't—mustn't make a messy. Mr. De-*Meanie* wouldn't like that."

"Ms. Stewart. Have you been drinking?" Damon asked, his handsome features closed in displeasure.

She screwed up her face to think. Why was thinking so hard? "Let's see..." She tapped her nose. "Have you been drinking..." She shook her head. "Yes, I have. I always have a glass of Pine-ippi-poop..." She stopped, squinted in thought. "Pippie-pini-puce..." She couldn't help herself, and burst out laughing. "Pipple-poopie..." Still tittering, she shrugged. "What was the question?"

Damon's mouth set grimly, he looked at her for a long moment. When he spoke, his accusation was edged with steel. "Blast it, Ms. Stewart, you're drunk."

Affronted by such slander, her spine went ramrod stiff. "How daaaaaare you—you..." Throwing up her hands in offense, she almost upended herself. "I don't have to *land* here and *stisten* to this!" With considerable effort controlling her motor skills, she managed to do little more than remain erect. With effort, she got her body to begin a disdainful turn, but lost her balance on the unsteady deck. She instinctively grabbed for a handhold, missed, and went sprawling to her knees.

"*Damn it,* Stewart!" Damon grasped her arm and hoisted her up. She gaped drunkenly at him. He was so tall—at least fifteen feet tall. And he sounded as though he was talking through a megaphone. She scrunched up her eyes to try to better make out his face. He was quite handsome, for a bully, even so far away. She was sorry he was such a bad, bad boy. "Hi," she breathed. "How's the weather up there, big guy?" She burst into a fit of giggles.

"Can you walk?" he asked.

"Suuuuuure. Been doin' it for years," she assured him with a nonchalant wave as she drooped back to her knees. "No—problem."

She felt herself being lifted away from the deck and sighed with the exhilarating rush she felt—like going up, up, up on a Ferris wheel. "Wheeeeee," she squealed, grabbing at something solid. When she looked more closely, she realized she was clutching Damon De-Morney's substantial neck. That neck was attached to a lovely square jaw. She scrutinized that jaw, sniffing. He smelled like a clean, summer night. Snuggling closer, she allowed her gaze to roam upward. After a moment of regarding his strong-boned face, she declared, "You have a teeny-weeny scar on your bottom lip."

He was frowning. "Thank you for that bulletin."

She traced the scar with her finger. It was hardly noticeable. "Kissy, kissy, make it aaaaaaall better," she whispered, then brushed his mouth with hers. As their lips met, she registered an odd tingling warmth rush through her body, a strange sensation, but nice. They'd been moving somewhere. Suddenly they weren't moving anymore. She drew away, sighing. "Whew! It's hot in here." There seemed to be something different in his eyes, but she couldn't quite tell what it was. She squinted, looking closer. "Are you hot, Damie? I'm reaaaaal hot."

He cleared his throat and muttered brusquely, "I'm locking up the cooking sherry."

They were moving again. She grinned up at him. "And did you knooooooow," she went on, tracing his lip, "that when you're mad your teeny-weeny scar turns white. Teeny-weeny white baby scar. How did you hurt yourself?" Her eyes lolled back to focus on his green gaze, now flashing with exasperation. "Noooo, don't tell me. Let me guess. You were scuba-duba diving and you attacked a shark that was littler than yooooou." Her giggle took her as much by surprise as it did the man carrying her. "Big, bad, sharkie, Damon De-Great White."

"I see you read the *Wall Street Journal*," he muttered.

"I looooove to read," she giggled, hugging him close. "You know what I don't like, though?"

"Sobriety?"

"Right." She shook her head. "Lobsters. I *hate* them. You know why? 'Cause we have to cook 'em alive. I always cried when I had to murder a lobster at ol' C.I.A." A torrent of desolation engulfed her and she blinked back tears. "I—I told Auntie Jo I couldn't do that. I can't murder any more lobsters. They scream. Did you know that? I can't. I just can't!" She clutched his shoulders, pleading, "Don't make me *off* any more lobsters!"

"I'll put in a call to the governor."

She wiped away a tear and, with trembly lips, smiled. "Good—reprieve all the lobsters."

Her hips touched something heavenly. Clouds?

"You may let go of me now, Ms. Stewart."

Mercy looked about her, not recognizing her surroundings. "Where am I? Dead?"

"No, but you may wish you were in a few hours," he replied with a heavy sigh. "This is my suite."

She blinked, taking note of the elegance of the bedroom. It was true. She was in the yacht's master suite, lounging on the oversize island bed. Dramatic hidden spotlights muted and warmed the luxurious decor of earth tones—rich greens and browns. A bank of large windows loomed before her, giving the suite a panoramic view of dark, choppy seas.

Disoriented and confused, she turned to frown into Mr. DeMorney's eyes, so near her face. They were wonderful eyes, even narrowed as they were. Was he angry, or troubled? She shook her head, feeling muddled. "What did you say?" she mumbled, wondering why her lips refused to work properly.

"You may let go of me now. You're safe on my bed," he repeated slowly as though she were a two-year-old.

She sluggishly snaked her hands away from his shoulders, peering about the opulent suite. Low, seductive music was playing somewhere, seeming to enfold the bed in blatant sensuality.

She became still, instantly suspicious. Mr. DeMorney had sounded a little short of breath. Was it unbridled passion? Was this master playboy seducing her? The *cad!* She lifted a foot and placed it squarely against his chest. "Mr. De-moo-moo. I'm no babe in the turnip truck. I'm twenty-twooooo. I've heard of sexual harmony-ment—er—harass-mony—uh..."

"Harassment," he corrected thinly. "So have I."

"You admit it—you brute! Shamey-shaaaaame on you!" In a shocked whisper, she asked, "Do you reeeeeeeally think your *body* will buy my *money?*" She winced. Had that come out right?

He straightened to his full height. With a shake of his silvery head, he looked down at her, his expression closed. "I don't expect you to understand this, in your condition, but since I don't know which of the crew's quarters belowdecks is yours, I brought you here. When you've sobered up, I hope you don't remember this conversation—for your own sake. For now, I suggest you sleep it off."

"Sweet talk will do you no good," she chided with a superior smirk. Lounging back on unsteady elbows, she demanded, "Now, I must ask you to get out before I call the poli-pice!" She flung out an arm, toppling on her side. "I'm *stummed* at you for trying to seduce my personal—person. I am a woman on a mission. I can't be bought!"

He pursed his lips. "I'm sure that's a commendable trait in a dipsomaniac." He regarded her for a moment, his expression going pensive, almost compassionate. Then, with an impatient oath, his brows drew together in a fierce scowl. "Ms. Stewart. You're fired."

She frowned, bewildered. When she'd blinked a couple of times, he was gone. She struggled up to a sitting position. Numbly she scanned the room with eyes that could no longer focus. Why was she sprawled in Damon DeMorney's suite? Had he actually been there a minute ago, or had she imagined it? And most worrisome of all, why did she have a heavy feeling in her gut—as though she'd just failed something or somebody? Shaking her head, she sank to her back. Well, at least she wasn't seasick.

MERCY SAT UP with a start. She had a pounding headache, and she'd just had the worst nightmare of her life! She'd dreamed that for some demented reason she'd actually kissed Damon DeMorney. Then she'd soundly chastised *him* for making advances on her, and thrown him out of her room!

Rubbing her eyes, she swung her legs over the side of her bed, or at least tried to. But there was no side. Her legs were still flat on the bed. Befuddled, she glanced about. Her confusion increased as she discovered she was sitting on a huge bed, a bed that was anchored in the middle of an equally huge bedroom.

She bit her lip as she scanned the place. The walls were a warm, paneled teakwood with mirrored inserts. To her right she saw a set of tall, beveled-glass-fronted bookshelves beside a built-in entertainment system. To her left, between a couple of doors, sat a beige sofa.

There was an expensive-looking stone Egyptian head mounted in a backlit alcove behind her, and on various built-in chests located about the room, there were striking metal sculptures. She glanced up. The ceiling was solid brass so highly polished she could see her own baffled expression. Lowering her gaze, she stared directly ahead out a wide expanse of curved windows to see the yacht's bow dipping and rising in a buffeting, white-capped sea. She swallowed, feeling a creeping unease snake up her spine. There was no getting around it. This was definitely the yacht's master suite.

The bed upon which she lounged was covered in a heavy green-on-green embossed silk. Scrambling from the mattress, she edged toward a door that stood ajar. Pushing it open, she discovered one of the two master bedroom heads. The room was lined with deep green marble, countertops, Jacuzzi tub and all. Cabinetry was polished teak, and the basin and fixtures were gold. She gasped at the opulence of it, then backed out. How had she gotten here?

With a fearful weakness engulfing her limbs, she sank onto the settee. *Oh, my Lord,* her mind cried as memories began to flood back. It hadn't been a nightmare at all. She'd actually...

She groaned, placing her head in her hands. She really had *kissed* Damon DeMorney. *And he really had fired her!*

Lifting teary eyes to stare unseeingly at the raging ocean, she had to admit she couldn't blame him. She shouldn't have taken Malcolm's pill. Obviously she'd had a bad reaction to it.

Her stomach knotted with devastation by all she'd lost because of a stupid mistake. Halfheartedly, she blinked to clear her vision, focusing on her watch. It was six o'clock. Dinner should have been started an hour ago. And fired or not, the captain and crew—and onboard tyrant—had to eat. With a wretched exhale, she pushed up and then was very sorry she had. She wasn't feeling well. The pill had worn off, and seasickness was overtaking her again.

She supposed she'd have to resort to Dramamine. Hiccups at least left her with her mental capacities intact. As soon as she got dinner on, she promised herself she'd seek out Damon DeMorney and apologize. She could just imagine his ire, and didn't relish facing him. Ever since she'd seen that arrogant, handsome face, she'd wanted nothing else but to get as far away from him and her foolhardy lie as she could. But for her grandfather's sake, she couldn't allow herself to be a coward, couldn't just run away. She had to try to finish this thing once and for all.

Her idea had seemed so right and uncomplicated in the beginning. She would simply get hired by the DeMorneys as chef, then dig out the truth and clear her grandfather's name. Now she was going to have to go crawling to Mr. DeMorney asking for a second chance—a chance that, if granted, might eventually cause *his* downfall.

On top of her seasickness, she was starting to feel a heaviness in her heart. She wasn't in the habit of deceiving people, *especially* with the intent to do them mischief.

She forced herself to think about sweet, fragile Otis—cheated out of so very much, lied about and disgraced. That image stiffened her spine and her resolve. Right after dinner she would face Mr. DeMorney and ask for her job back—*beg* if she had to.

The galley was abaft of the master suite, not far away. She hurried to it as quickly as her queasy stomach would allow. When she reached the door she was met with the aroma of chicken cacciatore. Even in her weakened condition, her trained nose told her it would taste delicious. Pushing open the door, she was startled to see Damon standing there, clad in the same blue shorts and shirt he'd had on during their ruinous encounter three hours ago. He was slicing vegetables into a salad bowl.

At the sound of her entry, he glanced over his shoulder and scanned her with a critical eye. Mercy swallowed, tamping down a feeling of culpability, and closed the door at her back.

"How are you feeling?" he asked.

It startled her that he cared, considering he'd been reduced to helping with dinner because he thought his chef was a drunkard. She met his gaze with difficulty. Her head was pounding and her stomach had known better moments. Nevertheless, this had to be said and it had to be said now if she hoped to remain on the DeMorney staff. "I—I want to apologize, sir. I acted abominably earlier. But I can explain."

He reached up into a cabinet over the counter where he was working. Lifting out a small bottle, he handed it to her. "Here. Take one of these. It'll help."

She eyed the bottle with distrust, considering her track record with pills lately. "What is it?"

"It's the same thing Malcolm gave you, but half the dosage. The scuttlebutt of your escapade in the pilothouse spread quickly, Ms. Stewart. When Malcolm heard about it he came to me and told me he'd given you some of his seasickness pills. I called his doctor in Miami, and he said, for a woman of your size, you were overmedicated. He prescribed a half dosage."

She opened the lid and shook out a pill. It was, in fact, half a pill. "Who broke these?" she asked.

"I did."

Her gaze shot to meet his. He was frowning, but it didn't seem to be aimed at her. "Look, Ms. Stewart," he began gravely. "I misjudged you this afternoon. I'm sorry."

"You—you mean I'm not fired?" She was stunned by this turn of events.

One corner of his mouth lifted, but it wasn't a happy expression. "I don't fire people for taking seasick medication."

A great weight was lifted off her shoulders. She wouldn't have to beg and grovel after all. "I appreciate it, sir," she said, experiencing an odd niggling of guilt. She hadn't expected him to actually be—nice.

With a warning lift of a brow, he cautioned, "It wasn't very bright of you to take medicine prescribed for a man who weighs two hundred and thirty pounds. I'd wager you weigh half that."

She decided it would be unwise of her ever to bet against Damon DeMorney. She weighed exactly half that. Embarrassed, she nodded. "Yes—it was pretty dumb." She didn't add that she had been desperate to find something to make her feel well enough to do her job. For a man who had just guessed her weight to the ounce, he probably realized that.

"Better take a pill," he reminded.

Without meeting his gaze, she walked to the sink and, fetching a glass from the cabinet, downed the medicine with some water.

"Hopefully, on the correct dosage, you won't be so willing to make my scars better," he remarked at her back.

She blushed fiercely at his reminder that she'd kissed him. *How could she have been so stupid! Clearly one of the most sinister side effects of overmedicating on this seasick prescription was a temporary loss of sanity.* Curling her hands around the edge of the sink, she whispered, "I—I'm terribly sorry about that, Mr. De-Morney."

"Did your parents kiss your hurts to make them better?"

The somber way he'd asked the question surprised her and she turned to face him. "Of course. Didn't yours?"

His nostrils flared, as though she'd slapped him. He shifted his gaze to pick up a carrot. "Where are your parents now?"

She noticed he'd shifted the subject back to her, but decided not to mention it. "They died when I was fifteen—house fire. My grandfather—er—" She stopped herself. She'd just gotten out of trouble with this man. All she needed to do now was reveal the Big Lie! Realizing she'd better at least finish her thought so he wouldn't start wondering why she hadn't, she said, "My grandpa kissed the hurts away, too." She added silently, *And now I'm trying to ease a hurt for him that your family caused!*

"Where is your grandfather?" Damon asked, slicing a carrot into the bowl.

"Mr. DeMorney, please," she prompted, disconcerted that she'd completely failed in her duties this evening. "I should be doing that."

"You cut up the radishes." He indicated the last uncut vegetables.

Worrying the inside of her cheek, she moved up beside him and silently began to slice radishes. The yacht was pitching fore and aft as it split the rampaging ocean waves. In order to keep from falling, Mercy braced her legs shoulder-width apart. One of her sneakers accidentally butted up against Damon's. For some reason she resisted drawing her foot away. She hoped he didn't take any particular notice of the contact, but touching the solidness of his body made her feel more secure somehow. The last thing she wanted to do was tumble to the floor. Not after the fiasco of this afternoon. She'd made enough of a fool of herself for one day.

"Tell me about your grandfather, Ms. Stewart," Damon said, interrupting her unruly train of thought.

His mellow, woodsy aftershave invaded her nostrils and became a pleasant addition to the aromas surrounding her. Forcing herself to concentrate on her work rather than the fact that her worst enemy was so pleasant-smelling and comfortingly stable, she offered minimally, "Grandpa's in a rest home in Iowa." Wanting to get off that volatile subject, and curious about something Aunt Jo had let slip about his family—something unhappy—she asked, "What about your folks?"

His fingers stilled in their action of slicing. "Gone. Boating accident when I was ten. But we weren't close."

She inspected his profile. His features had become hard, his tone tight. He looked as though he didn't plan to discuss it further. Taking the broad hint, she veered to a question she felt might be safer. "Who made the cacciatore?"

"I did."

She was surprised, assuming it had been one of the stewardesses. "You?"

Dropping the last carrot slice into the salad, he wiped his hands on a towel. "Some men do cook."

"Oh, I know that. Some of the best chefs are men. I—I just didn't know— I mean, you head up a big car company. I didn't think you'd have time to cook."

"I don't have as much time as I'd like. But I enjoy cooking."

She glanced around, noticing for the first time that the galley was spotless. Apparently her expression mirrored her surprise, for he chuckled deeply. "It is possible to cook without wreaking havoc on the galley."

His remark stung. She couldn't tell if he'd meant to be condescending or not, but it fired her anger. Hard-pressed to keep a civil tongue in her mouth, yet mindful that she'd already been fired once today, she said only, "Temperaments differ, Mr. DeMorney. My method may be initially more—uh—maladroit—but in the end, we get the same results. A good meal and a clean galley."

He half grinned. "Maladroit? That's a very pretty word, but it still means sloppy."

Was he trying to provoke her? "What are you telling me, sir? Must I do it your way to remain employed here?"

He finished slicing the last carrot. Putting the knife down, he planted one hand on the countertop and leaned toward her. Their faces were inches apart, and Mercy suddenly felt overwarm. She could see that little scar on his lip very clearly, and realized she was blushing with the memory of his mouth pressed against hers. She prayed that the same thought wasn't going through his mind.

His expression didn't give much away, merely seemed inquiring. "Tell me, Ms. Stewart," he began, his breath teasing her cheek, "have you actually brought up Aunt Jo's estrogen levels or is that one of her fanciful dreams that you're just going along with?"

Thrown off by his sudden closeness and abrupt topic change, Mercy frowned, faltering, "Why—why, no. It's no fanciful dream. The *British Medical Journal* had an article about a recent study where a group of women between fifty and seventy—"

"You read the *British Medical Journal?*" he broke in, his features easing into a skeptical grin.

The dashing smile sent a dither of mixed emotions dancing through her. On the one hand, she was affronted by the obvious incredulity of his question, as though he thought she couldn't read anything more enlightening than a recipe book. On the other hand, that flash of perfect teeth, coupled with the sexy sparkle in his eyes, made her insides quiver with female excitement. Since Damon DeMorney was her archenemy, it wasn't a good combination of emotions to feel, for she dared not act on either response if she hoped to accomplish her scheme.

Very conscious of his searching gaze, and smarting from feeling any attraction at all for him, Mercy sacrificed a need to voice a scathing retort. Clearing her throat, she counted to ten to calm herself. "I found the *British Medical Journal* among the magazines at my dentist's office," she informed him. "I happened to have a long wait that day, so I read it."

He nodded, his grin wry, but undeniably charming. "Well, then, for Aunt Jo's flourishing estrogen level, I'll try to ignore the majority of your maladroitness."

You're too kind! she screamed silently, though outwardly she smiled back. "Why, thank you so much, Mr. DeMorney." It had come out strained. The sudden fading of Damon's grin told her he'd detected her contempt. She toyed uneasily with her lower lip. Was there nothing she could get by this intuitive man? *There'd bet-*

ter be, she scolded herself. *Or you'll fail Grandpa and never get his name cleared!*

THE NEXT DAY, the seas had grown calmer—an undulating palette of blues and greens basking beneath a bright October sun. It was midafternoon, and since dinner wasn't going to be complicated, Mercy decided to try a gutsy move. Her grandfather had been asking for a picture of Damon and her together. Naturally there was no way she could do that, but she thought she might be able to sneak a quick snapshot of him.

Not long ago she'd heard him exit his shipboard office with its specially outfitted satellite communications center. He'd spent most of the cruise cloistered away there, wheeling and dealing and shouting, "Off with their heads," she supposed. She'd peeked down the hall to watch as he went out onto the covered aft deck to enjoy the first sunshine of the cruise.

With her inexpensive camera clutched in her fist, she headed through the salon toward the double smoked-glass doors that led there. She hoped he'd be standing out by the railing. That way she could take a picture through a crack between the doors and he'd never know about it.

She peered out. Good. There he was, beyond a shaded lounge area made up of elegant wicker furniture and a slate-topped table. He was near the railing, scanning the sea.

Today he was wearing white shorts and a green crew-neck shirt. His hair shone like melted silver in the sun, and his shoulders seemed too wide for even such a tall man to bear comfortably. Her gaze drifted to his classically handsome profile—the straight nose, jutting cheekbones and strong, stubborn chin.

He was frowning, in deep concentration. It would have been better if she could have caught him smiling. But those moments were few and far between, since he spent most of his time either in his office or with dark thoughts on his mind. Yet even with his features locked in a perpetual scowl, he was painfully handsome. With an irritating flutter in her breast, she raised the camera to snap the shot.

As she did, he turned in her direction. Squinting to better probe the relative darkness, he moved to lounge against the rail. "What are you doing?" he called rather gruffly.

Lord, he must have the ears and eyes of—of Superman! "I—I was just…" Realizing she had no choice, she stepped out onto the deck, lifting her camera. "I was just taking a picture of—of the scenery." It was only half a lie, she told herself. There would have been *scenery* in the picture, too.

His features grew dubious as he plunged his hands into his pockets and crossed his ankles. He relaxed there silently for a long moment, in a classy slouch straight out of the pages of some slick gentlemen's magazine. While she took a long, calming breath, he finally said, "The scenery is empty ocean, Ms. Stewart."

She winced, wishing she were a more experienced liar. "I know. It's just that I grew up in—er—a little town in Kansas." That was a lie. She'd never set foot in Kansas. But she'd heard it was flat there. "The ocean looks like the land around Prairie Village. Flat as far as the eye can see." She was thinking fast, maybe too fast, but she hurried on. "Except, of course, from Prairie Village the view's not water, it's—uh..."

"Prairie?" he helped, with a somewhat skeptical quirk of his lips.

Her cheeks blazed. "Something like that, yes."

"Do you want a picture for your grandfather?" he asked, startling her so badly she feared he'd figured out her entire nefarious plot. But when she gave herself a second to think about it, she knew it would be natural for her to want to send her ailing grandfather a few pictures. Inhaling to steady her voice, she said, "Why—why, yes."

"Let me take one with you in it."

That wasn't quite what she wanted. "Okay—if you let me get one of you."

A brow arched inquiringly. "Me?"

She lifted a shoulder, hoping the movement looked unconcerned. "I think my grandfather would like to see who I work for. I've already got lots of shots of Josephine and her pigs." *Finally, the truth, for a change.*

He strolled the long distance to where she was standing, taking her camera. "I'm sure he'd rather have one of you." Motioning toward the railing above the fishing cockpit, he said, "Stand over there in the sun."

She did as he asked, but didn't feel much like smiling. Maybe he didn't enjoy having his picture taken unless some drop-dead beauty was hanging on his arm. Well, she supposed she'd just have to try to sneak a picture, again, some other time.

"Smile, Ms. Stewart. You look like a poster to save the whooping cranes."

She forced a cheerful grin.

After he'd snapped the picture, he joined her by the railing. "There you go." Stretching out a strong, bronzed hand, he handed her back her camera. "I hope your grandfather likes it."

"You're sure I can't get a shot of you?" she tried halfheartedly.

"I don't take a good picture, Ms. Stewart."

She gave up with a shrug. "That's true. Photographs don't do you justice."

His chuckle startled her. "They don't?"

She snapped her glance to his face. *Had she actually said that out loud?* She sidled away along the rail, unnerved by his looming, amused presence. "Well—you're no simpleton, Mr. DeMorney," she retorted in her own defense. "I'm sure you know by now you're—rather good-looking." *For a self-important, egotistical tyrant!*

His sparkling eyes held hers, and she chafed beneath his speculation. "Do you think I'm good-looking, Ms. Stewart?" His lips quirked wryly.

She shuddered with humiliation. He was toying with her. "Some women would say so. P-personally, I prefer dark men," she fibbed.

His eyes alight with mirth, he queried, "You do?"

She nodded, edging farther away. He was doing nothing overt to alarm her, merely standing there with his hands in his pockets, looking terribly alluring. He wasn't even smiling, not really. But she was feeling—not quite threatened—but something! How could his simply standing there answering her questions with questions, and watching her with those sparkling emerald eyes, upset her so? *Good grief!* She felt as though she were about to be devoured whole. What was worse, the experience was both thrilling and frightening at once. "I—I'd better be going," she managed weakly.

"Then I won't keep you, Ms. Stewart."

He was openly laughing at her now. At least his eyes were. She wheeled away, feeling like an utter dolt.

"Ms. Stewart," he called as she was about to escape through the double doors. She halted, loath to turn back, but knowing she must.

Letting the doors slip from her fingers, she reluctantly faced him. "Yes, sir?" she asked, her voice an awkward squeak.

He cocked his silvery head, indicating that she should come back.

On unwilling feet, she did as she was instructed. "What is it, Mr. DeMorney?" She wondered miserably if his plan was to keep up his mockery until he drove her to tears.

His gaze, narrowed by the brightness of the sun, was unreadable, but the grin he flashed was unexpectedly friendly. "What the hell. Take the damned picture for your grandfather. Anyone who'd kiss the hurts away, I'd probably like."

She was so shocked, it took her a few seconds of fumbling before she could get the camera to her face. Espying him through the viewfinder, she began to suffer an unanticipated bout of guilt. Here he was, being obliging, leaning against the railing, grinning at her, thinking he was doing a sick old man a kindness. And what was she going to do with his picture? She was going to send it along to her grandfather with the barefaced lie, *Here's my wonderful husband, Damon.*

Snapping this photo was the most deceitful thing she'd done so far. Though she knew she was right in being here, right in trying to clean the stain from her grandfather's reputation, she suddenly didn't like herself very much.

"Is there a problem, Ms. Stewart? You seem—"

"No!" she cried. With a surge of self-preservation, she amended with less shrillness, "Er—not at all."

She snapped the picture. Lowering the camera, she found it impossible to look him in the eye. Even if he were a sleaze, she didn't like the idea that she just might be stooping to his level. "It—it was fine, Mr. DeMorney. Thanks." Mumbling something vague about needing to get back to the galley, she whirled away and fled.

CHAPTER THREE

THE NEXT DAY, Mercy watched from the window of her galley as Captain Meyers docked the *Silver Cat* at the DeMorneys's private pier behind his Grand Cayman hideaway.

A blossom-scented sea breeze wafted through the window, and she inhaled the sweet air, feeling her spirits rise in spite of the strain of her secret.

She scanned the panorama before her. It was unlike any October day she could recall in her life. A white beach glistened as water, tinted azure in a noontime sun, lapped languidly across it. About thirty feet back from the sea, the scenery grew dense and tropical, exhibiting a wild profusion of green things growing in erratic and indecisive loveliness.

The wall of ferns and palm trees was broken in one spot by what appeared to be a narrow walkway made of broken shells. It was bordered on either side by red azaleas that spilled over onto the path that meandered out of sight into the equatorial shadows. Bent shanks of hundreds of palms, red mangrove and wild bamboo guarded any evidence that a house existed within its lush custody, and Mercy, even as nervous as she was, became curious about what lurked within the hushed forest.

There was a hustle and bustle outside her galley window as Malcolm and a couple other members of the crew tied up the yacht. Mercy turned away from the window and scanned the galley. It sparkled. There was not a single thing left to do. She began to wonder how she'd keep occupied while they were docked. One of the more gossipy stewardesses, Bonnie Smith, had said the Grand Cayman house was kept staffed year-round, so there would be little for the *Silver Cat*'s crew to do while they were tied up.

Mercy wasn't pleased about that. She needed to keep herself occupied so her thoughts wouldn't be tormented every minute by the fact that Otis's life was ticking away while she stood idle, doing nothing to help clear his reputation.

Bonnie had also told her this island house had been in the DeMorney family for over thirty years. She doubted there would be any business files or books stored here, but she vowed she'd keep her eyes and ears open. If she was lucky, maybe the trip wouldn't be a total waste of time.

With a sigh, she realized she might as well go ashore. At her first opportunity she'd ask Mr. DeMorney if she could help with the cooking in the main house. That would be better than doing nothing, she supposed.

When she reached the foyer that led to the deck, she heard a door open, and reflexively turned. There stood Damon, just leaving his office. He was clad in white cotton slacks and a white shirt that made his light-colored hair seem even more dazzling than usual. The striking visual feast gave her pause, but she tried to hide that fact.

He watched her thoughtfully for a moment before he acknowledged her with a brief nod. She nodded, too, not sure what else she might be expected to do. Applaud? Kiss his ring? Why did one simple glance from him make her so nervous and unsure of herself? She felt antsy. Needing to move, do something, she stuffed a stray wisp of hair behind her ear.

Patting the strand into place, she decided to take the initiative. If she wanted to be busy to keep her mind off—things—this was as good a time as any to ask. "Mr. DeMorney, I've been wondering what you expect of me while we're on Grand Cayman?"

He indicated the exit. "Why don't we walk while we talk," he remarked, startling her.

"Oh, I—don't mean to be a bother if you're in a hurry," she demurred.

A tired smile tipped one corner of his mouth. "I'm in no great hurry."

He surprised her again by holding the door for her. She stepped out onto the yacht's sunny deck, then preceded him down the metal gangway. They didn't speak again until they'd trod the entire length of the fifty-foot dock and were descending the stone steps to the beach.

"It's lovely," she observed out loud, finding the boundless beauty of the place required an open admission.

"I hadn't noticed." His voice had been low and seemed vaguely troubled.

She peered at him. "How could you not notice? It's like heaven."

"It was my parents' home."

After a tense pause, she asked, "You didn't live here with them?"

"Not long." He nodded toward the path. "This way."

She watched him covertly as he strode toward the walkway. He hadn't lived with his family very long? "Did you visit—"

"No," he cut in, his shortness implying the subject was off-limits.

It was clear he wasn't happy. She didn't know if his troubled expression was because he didn't like this place and its memories, or if he was merely anticipating trouble with his board meeting. "Ms. Stewart," he added less sternly. "In answer to your original question. The staff here is quite complete. Why don't you consider this week a paid vacation."

She couldn't think of a thing to say. She knew he would expect her to be grateful. Most employees would be thrilled to be given a vacation with pay in a tropical paradise like this. But she was immediately filled with gloom. Though she offered a wan smile in answer, to her this so-called vacation would be just one more squandered week where she would be unable to get at those all-important company books. "That's great," she managed, swallowing to ease the prickly dryness of frustration in her throat.

They stepped onto the path of shells. It made a pleasant crunching sound with their tread, but was so narrow that Mercy had to precede Damon. She squinted, trying to adjust her eyes to the dimness.

There was a rustling, and she ducked, fearful. "What was that?"

"Parrots," Damon said. "Look. There." He indicated the direction of the dock. Through the spread fingers of palmettos she watched as two deep green birds, their color very like Damon's eyes, winged away along the beach. "There are hummingbirds along the path, too, so don't faint if you run into a swarm of them. They're harmless."

Her eyes were adjusting now, and she peered at him, irked at his patronizing tone. "Thanks for the warning," she mumbled, her jaws tight.

"By your tone, Ms. Stewart, I assume you believe I was being condescending," he said, offering a token smile. "I apologize."

He'd sounded more preoccupied than contrite, making her doubt that he cared all that much. Though she forced herself to smile back, she had a rebellious urge to suggest that he couldn't help being condescending, being the smug, self-important tyrant that he was, but she restrained herself. "Forget it," she muttered. Turning away, she decided to ignore him and began to inspect the cool retreat through which she walked.

After a quiet moment of ambling along the path that wound around between the curved shanks of giant palms, she smiled a genuine smile at the unstudied beauty of the tunnel-like pathway. Gazing upward, high in the feathery branches of the tropical trees, everything was in motion. As she gazed at nature's rustling dance, she found herself somewhat calmed by the unspoiled loveliness. "Why—it's wonderful. I've never seen anyplace so—so peaceful."

"A matter of opinion, I suppose," he replied, surprising her with his closeness. She hadn't realized she'd halted, blocking the path. Feeling flushed, and unsure why, she scurried on.

Farther along, the sky brightened, and Mercy realized they were reaching a manicured lawn. The crunchy walkway exited the jungle flora and brought them bit by bit into courtly civilization through a bright tangle of roses, camellia, periwinkle, thick ferns and adroitly placed boulders. Hummingbirds flitted about the multitude of blossoms, looking like playful storybook fairies.

At the path's end, Mercy halted. Beyond the garden, a pair of ancient sea grape trees framed a view of a long, low house, its architecture hinting of both Italy and Southern California. Scarlet bougainvillea scaled its mellowed stone walls and clambered along the red slate roof.

Nestled in artfully landscaped wide-leafed foliage, the house's rear facade showcased a shaded, airy terrace, its square columns choked with vining roses. An oval swimming pool, tranquil and mirrorlike, was to the left of the terrace. Camellia, jasmine and white azaleas bordered a tunnel-shaped, latticework pergola that lined the residence on that side, keeping the forest from encroaching onto the lawn.

On the other side of the house, the lawn, dotted with huge, bowed palms interspersed with decorative mango and almond trees, ran for quite some distance before a stone wall separated it from neighboring junglelike foliage that would engulf everything if left to itself.

This was the sort of idyllic solitude Mercy had only dreamed existed. She couldn't imagine anyone having the good fortune to live in a place like this. Turning a stunned expression on Damon, she whispered, "How could you dislike such a beautiful place?"

He half smiled, but it wasn't a happy expression. Taking her arm, he said, "It must be nice to be so naive, Ms. Stewart."

She stared at him as he turned her toward the house. She had a sudden flash, a realization. Unable to help herself, she asked, "This is where your family died, isn't it?"

He stiffened, turning toward her. Something flashed in his eyes, but it came and went so rapidly she couldn't guess what the dark emotion was—hatred? Pain? Anger? With nostrils flaring, he warned harshly, "I will not tolerate these continued intrusions into my personal life, Ms. Stewart."

His fingers tightened around her arm in his irritation and she swallowed, recognizing she'd gone too far. His family's problems were none of her business. Feeling badly for blurting such a personal question, she said, "I—I'm sorry, Mr. De—"

"Did you have any other questions—about your *duties* while you're here?" he cut in, his tone ominous.

It was clear he didn't intend to discuss the matter, even if it was only to accept her apology. She took his unspoken direction. "Where will the crew be staying, sir?" she murmured.

"Mrs. Brownly, my housekeeper, will—"

"Messy Miss!" came a hoarse cry, drawing both Mercy's and Damon's attention. Hearing her grandpa Goodeve's pet name for her, she swirled toward the sound to see movement on the shadowed terrace. It couldn't be her grandfather! But nobody else in the world

had ever called her that name. Gulping back the bitter bile of looming discovery, she could only stare in stark panic. *Please! Please say it isn't so!* she prayed silently. *He can't be here. He's too sick—too deathly ill! This will kill him!*

Mercy's heart dropped as she watched the unthinkable happen—a familiar, thin image was tottering toward her, leaning heavily on a cane. Even in the deep shadows she recognized her grandfather's kindly, gaunt face, hawk nose, and the sheen of his balding pate. Mercy cast Damon an apprehensive look. He, too, was watching her grandfather's labored approach.

"Messy Miss?" Damon asked. "Obviously the man knows your style of cooking, but who is he?"

Mercy gulped hard. All she needed now was her boss's sarcasm. "It's my grandfather," she whispered.

"I thought you said your grandfather was in a rest home."

Otis beckoned feebly. "Come—come here, Mercy. Give me a hug," Otis rasped. "And you, too, Damon, my boy. Let me hug my brand-new son-in-law."

The blood drained from Mercy's face. She twisted toward her employer, sure he could read the panic in her eyes. Grasping both his hands in hers, she pleaded under her breath, "Mr. DeMorney, I can explain. Before you say anything, *please* go along. My grandfather thinks we're married. He's very ill, and any shock could *kill* him!"

Incredulous green eyes impaled her. "He thinks we're *what?*" Just moments ago he'd made it clear that he didn't tolerate intrusions into his personal life. By his brutal expression, she sensed he felt exceedingly intruded upon right now.

Towering over her as he was, Mercy felt about two inches tall. If he'd wanted to, he could have reached out and strangled her with one hand. His hard-edged expression told her he was considering it.

"Please!" she cried under her breath. "I'll get him on the first plane out of here! Just—go along for a few minutes!"

He flashed a quick glance over her shoulder toward the old man. "Ms. Stewart, are you nuts?"

"Probably." There was no time to argue or defend herself. She begged, "Quick, put your arm around me and wave."

Damon's expression was a mixture of disbelief, rage and frustration. "Why in hell would you tell him we're married?"

"Could you please save the inquisition until later?" she asked plaintively. Her heart hammered. Every second Otis was struggling closer to them. Though they were at least thirty feet from the terrace, and well out of earshot, she knew she only had seconds to get Damon to help her, or the game—her scheme—was up.

He'd clamped his jaws tight, making his cheek muscles stand out. Clearly he was far from won over.

"I promise he'll be out of here on the very next plane."

His expression was disapproving, but with one more glance at her grandfather, he seemed to relent slightly. "The next plane?" he demanded through gritted teeth.

She nodded, experiencing a flood of hope. Smiling and waving for the benefit of her grandfather, she asided,

"*Please* put your arm around me, Mr. DeMorney." Louder, she called, "Grandpa. What a nice surprise."

She quickened her step across the lawn, not wanting Otis to overtire himself. It startled her when an arm encircled her shoulder. A quick peek from the corner of her eye confirmed that Damon was going along. He was even waving.

"Thank you," she whispered, truly grateful. Even though she'd practically blackmailed him with images of her grandfather dropping dead on the lawn, she hadn't expected this much cooperation. She didn't even dare think about what she'd expected.

"What the hell is his name?" Damon demanded through a fake grin.

"Just call him Grandpa," she said, not sure if the name Otis would set off any warning bells in his brain or not, since her grandfather had been fired before Damon's birth.

If she could scoot her grandfather onto the first plane back to the States, she could still pull off her plan with nobody the wiser. Of course, Damon might fire her just for lying about being married to him. But she couldn't worry about that now. Her grandfather's health had to come first.

"Grandpa," she cried when she reached the terrace's edge. "I can't believe you're here." She hugged his frail shoulders, and he hugged her back. She inhaled the familiar scent of his inexpensive, musky aftershave. It was comforting. She wished she could have spent more time with him these past months, but the rest home was expensive, so she'd had to work. "What were you thinking, coming all this way?" she reprimanded softly.

He let her go and kissed her cheek, then turned to look up at Damon, his old, brown eyes twinkling. "Mercy— honey," he said through labored breaths. "Ever since you told me—about marrying this young buck, I've just felt better and better." He reached for Damon. "Let's have a hug—my boy."

Mercy stepped back, clasping nervous hands together as Damon allowed himself to be embraced by this total stranger.

He gave her a sidelong frown as he said, "It's good to meet you—Grandpa."

"It's like a dream come true, son." Otis patted Damon's powerful back as he clung to him for support.

Damon's frown deepened, his sharp gaze remaining on Mercy. "I'm happy you're feeling better."

Oh, dear! Mercy realized any second now Otis would say something about Damon's grandfather, Kennard, and her world would come crashing down around her. In a last-ditch effort to save her plan, her lie and her grandfather's health, she interjected, "Uh—Grandpa—Mr.— er—Damon has to—to make an important call. And you need to rest." She peeled his thin arms from her pseudo-husband, and pasted on a grin. "Why don't we let him make that call, and you and I can talk."

Biting nervously at her lip, she gestured toward the house with her head and shot Damon a *please go away!* look.

He gave her another accusing glance, then with a sur-prisingly believable smile, nodded toward Otis. "I'd better make that important call—Grandpa." Startling Mercy, he bent to brush his lips lightly across hers, mur-

muring, "Darling..." As he lifted his mouth away, he muttered near her ear, *"Get him out of here."*

THE LAST FLIGHT out of Grand Cayman was at nine that night. An eternity away. Mercy had been relieved to discover that all he'd told the housekeeper when he'd arrived was that he had a "big surprise" for Mr. DeMorney. She supposed she shouldn't be all that amazed that the housekeeper had let him in. Otis was such a sweet, irresistible old man. Still, she couldn't believe her luck that he hadn't said anything about "Mr. and *Mrs.* DeMorney." But that had only been a temporary reprieve.

She was beside herself about how to keep Otis away from everybody, especially Damon. There was no way Grandpa could be with Damon for even five minutes without saying something incriminating.

She'd taken him out and sat with him on the beach for a while, then talked him into a nice, long nap before dinner. But what was she going to do about dinner? He was sure to assume, as the grandfather of Damon's wife, he'd be expected to eat with them.

Mercy had been so upset by her grandfather's disturbing appearance, she hadn't brought her bags to shore, hadn't consulted Mrs. Brownly, the housekeeper, about her accommodations, hadn't taken off for Georgetown and souvenir shopping with the rest of the *Silver Cat*'s crew. She'd merely lurked near the guest room Mrs. Brownly had given to her grandfather for his nap, fearful that if she left even for a short time, he'd wake up, wander around and get himself—and her—into irreparable trouble.

So, she skulked in the sleek, white stucco hall. After a while, afraid her pacing might attract undue attention from servants, she perched on a long, contemporary rush bench, tapping her foot fretfully on the black granite floor, pretending to admire several abstract paintings that hung along the hallway wall—bright splashes of color cavorting across the canvas, giving a liveliness to the stark walls. In reality she wasn't so much into the art as she was into stealthily watching the second hand on her wristwatch mark the slow passing of time. There were six grueling hours left until the next flight back to Miami.

"Ms. Stewart," came the very distinctive voice of Damon DeMorney.

She jerked around to see him standing not far away and automatically jumped up to stand. "Yes, sir?"

He leaned against the wall, eyeing her dubiously. "I think you know what we need to discuss."

A chill of apprehension skittered along her spine. "Yes, sir, I think—I do." She eyed the door to the room where her grandfather napped, worrying the inside of her cheek. "It's just that I don't think I should go very far away—in case he should get up and decide to wander around."

Damon indicated the glass patio doors at his back. "You can watch from out there."

She had to agree. They'd have privacy as well as a view of the hallway. Dreading this conversation, she headed toward the patio. Damon fell into step beside her. When they reached the doors, he opened one for her to precede him. She felt a bit grudging about it. Why was he bothering to act the gentleman when he was just about to give her the ax? Did he think he was being kind? On the contrary, he was just drawing out her anguish.

After they'd reached the cool, shaded patio, he indicated a seating area of redwood furniture covered in off-white linen. She took a seat at one end of the sofa while he sat down in an armchair positioned at a right angle to her. She had a hard time looking directly at him, so she focused on the rustic redwood coffee table before her. A large stone bowl in its center contained a gorgeous, red-blossomed tropical plant.

"Ms. Stewart," he began, "what you've done is quite serious."

She cast him a pained look. "I know that, sir."

He eyed her quizzically. "Why in heaven's name did you tell your grandfather such a lie?"

She squirmed, casting her glance away. It was very quiet, she realized, except for the constant twitter of birds. It seemed that winged creatures were everywhere, happily darting, calling and chattering, probably even gossiping about foolish young chefs who were on the verge of being fired. She had the absurd feeling they were gathering to get a better look.

"Why me, Ms. Stewart?" he asked, drawing her back. "Why didn't you tell your grandfather you'd married one of those dark men you prefer?"

He sat forward, templing his fingers, and merely looked at her, not appearing particularly bloodthirsty. Maybe she still had a chance to keep her job. She just had to come up with a believable story and play on his compassion. By going along with her lie earlier, he'd done a very compassionate thing, proving he wasn't totally im-

mune to compassion—at least when it came to the idea
of elderly men dropping dead in front of him.

She decided to give one more little fabrication a try.
"I—I lied because Grandpa, er, wanted to see me married and happy before he died. So, I guess—I just—" she
shrugged, finishing sheepishly "—picked you, since I was
working for you and all." Her cheeks burned. Oh, how
she wished she'd never started this charade. It seemed to
be getting worse and worse by the minute. *If only he'd
swallow this last little fib!*

He sat back, seeming to consider what she'd said.
When he faced her again, he asked, "What's wrong with
your grandfather?"

She sighed, despondent to be reminded of her grandfather's fragile health. "The doctor said he's just wearing out, giving up. He's had a—a hard life."

"I see." He scanned her face. "I'm sorry."

She was startled by his sympathy and wondered if it
was genuine. "Thank you," she murmured.

"So, you're going to send him back and allow him to
pass away believing we're married?"

She winced at his disapproving tone. "I didn't want
him to worry about me," she objected. "I didn't think it
would hurt."

"I appreciate your motives, Ms. Stewart. But you must
understand, I can't allow my employees to make a practice of telling sickly relatives I've married them merely to
ease their passing."

Dread, swift and hot, raced through her. Here it came.
He was firing her after all.

Just then she heard a noise and glanced beyond the
glass doors to see Otis emerging from his room. "Oh,

no," she moaned, jumping up. "It's Grandpa." Panicked, she looked down at her boss. "What should we do?"

He flicked a look toward the doors in time to see Otis spot them. Turning back to Mercy, he asked, "How long have we been married?"

She shrugged. "A couple of weeks."

He absorbed the information, looking exasperated. Surprising her, he took her hand and pulled her into his lap. "Then we'd be on our honeymoon."

She fell onto his thighs, able to do nothing more than stare at him.

"Which would you prefer," he asked, "that I kiss you or just gaze lovingly into your eyes?"

She found herself intensely aware of his sinuous maleness, so vital and warm beneath her hips. His scent filled her senses and his alluring green eyes, even narrowed with aggravation, made her heart race strangely. "Uh—I guess a loving look will do..." she said, her voice strained.

He encircled her waist with his arms, leaned close, his expression going gentle. The smoldering flame she saw spark to life in his eyes flabbergasted her. "How's this?" he queried near her mouth.

Even knowing this was a fake seduction, she experienced an unwelcome surge of attraction for him, and it took all her willpower to keep from moving that last inch to touch his lips with hers. "It's—it's just fine—sir...."
She had to force herself to turn and make sure her grandfather was making it okay. The smile she had commanded to her lips froze and then faded. "Oh—dear..." She breathed in a moan as Aunt Jo joined Otis just beyond the doors. While she helplessly stared, the elderly

woman hugged the old man and a host of strangers joined them.

Mercy opened her mouth to try to make some sense out of this turn of events, but didn't have time. The door was pushed open as the crowd spilled onto the patio. Aunt Jo trilled, "What a wonderful surprise! To discover that my naughty grandnephew has gone and married my kitchen angel behind my back!"

Damon twisted around.

"Who are those people?" Mercy cried under her breath, horrified to be caught in Damon's lap.

He muttered a dark oath. "It's my damned board of directors. The company plane must have arrived early."

She started to scramble up, but he held her fast. "Too late, Ms. Stewart," he muttered near her ear, suddenly grinning. She knew the expression was just as phony as his seductive look a moment ago, and she was confused.

"Why?" she asked.

"Save the inquisition for later, *darling,*" he warned, his tone grim.

She met his flinty gaze and her heart began to thud. What did that look mean? Before she had a chance to analyze or question it, he crushed her against his chest and kissed her so passionately she felt the earth cant dangerously on its axis then explode into millions of lovely, fiery fragments.

CHAPTER FOUR

THE KISS WAS HOT and lingering. Yet even when it ended Mercy was still dizzy, her heart skipping again and again. She'd never been kissed like that in her life. Suddenly, Damon's nearness was a staggeringly frightening experience. This man was her worst enemy, yet lightning bolts of unwanted excitement continued to dance through her. Against her will, she had to admit she found him disturbingly seductive. That revelation was even more disquieting since she knew he'd only been acting.

She wanted to jump up, to run away, but even if her legs had been steady enough to support her, she couldn't move, for he was holding her against him. Blinking, she stared up at his face, confused, wondering why he was restraining her. He was smiling, yet there was a vein throbbing in his temple that belied that pleasant expression. Mercy began to have an uneasy feeling that he was hatching some deceptive plan of his own.

A cluster of people was gathering around them, all talking at once. Some were smiling, some were not. One particular woman, Mercy noticed, wore a rather sour expression, marring her otherwise pretty features. But it was all such a blur.

There was Otis's pale, grinning face and Aunt Jo's flushed countenance as she patted first Mercy's cheek then her own heavy wig.

The first thing that rang completely clear in her mind was Aunt Jo's loud remark. "Otis, dear, it's been just too long since we've seen you. I always felt so badly about the unfortunate way you left the company."

Mercy stopped breathing. Josephine had blurted out her terrible secret! Her fearful gaze lurched to Damon's face. He was looking at her oddly now, as though he'd never seen her before. She felt a skittering unease, like a spider dashing along her spine. Was he becoming aware that there was more to Mercy's lie than merely letting her dear old grandfather go to his final reward in peace?

She felt herself being lifted to stand as Damon stood up and took her hand in his. When her glance darted to his face, again she noticed that he was smiling at the chattering group. "Aunt Jo and my housekeeper will see that you're all settled. I'm sure you understand that my bride and I want to be alone, so we'll be staying on the yacht." He gave Mercy a loving grin, though his eyes sparked with a less blissful emotion. "If you'll excuse us, we'll see you later."

After one last, damp kiss from Aunt Jo, Mercy found herself being hustled along the back lawn toward the jungle barrier. When they were out of earshot, she asked, "What's going on? Why did you let everybody think—"

"Why didn't you tell me your sweet, old grandfather was Otis Goodeve?" he interjected. Though he hadn't raised his voice, there was icy anger in his question.

She stumbled, but couldn't halt because he was fairly dragging her along. They entered the darkness of the forest, and she yanked on his hold, but to no avail. "I—I—" She drew a deep breath, working to control the tremor in her voice. "I didn't think it was any of your business," she tried, doubting that he'd buy that.

"You must think I'm an idiot," he growled, halting to glare down at her.

"Of course, I don't!" she retorted, smarting not only from the discomfort in her wrist but from the sharper pain of being found out before she'd managed to do one single thing to help her grandfather. "I never thought any such thing, Mr. DeMorney. But since you know who Grandpa is, I'll tell you what I *do* think. I think your grandfather was a *crook*. I think he swindled Grandpa out of what was rightfully his. That's what I think!"

His expression had gone so furious she couldn't help but wince, but she hurried on. "The truth is, I wanted to clear my grandfather's name before he died. That's why I applied for the job with your family." She lifted her head proudly. "Grandpa's so sweet-natured he thought he'd mistakenly done something wrong all those years ago. My mother told me over and over how sad he was, how badly he'd felt. She swore until her dying day that he never did anything deceitful. Grandpa wouldn't have wanted me to get involved. But I *know* he's innocent and I wanted to prove it, so I lied to him about being married to you—to keep him from worrying. Happy now?"

One tawny brow arched skeptically. "You little fool," he chided coldly, the very coldness of his tone dismaying. "Do you expect me to believe a wild accusation from one man's disgruntled, clearly prejudiced, daughter?"

"If you're so sure it's all that wild, then prove it. Order an audit going back to the very beginning—if you *dare!*" she challenged.

"Don't be ridiculous." He turned away and began to pull her toward the yacht again.

She was totally dumbfounded now. What in the world was he doing with her, allowing the marriage lie to go on? "Where are you dragging me?"

"To our honeymoon suite."

"Wh-what?" she panted as they exited the forest onto the beach. "I don't understand. Why are you doing this—especially now—now that you—"

"Now that I know what a conniving, lying phony you are?"

She bristled. "I'm no phony. I *am* a chef."

He laughed bitterly. "My mistake, you're a liar, a conniver *and* a chef."

"What do you intend to do with me? Make me walk the plank?" she asked as he tugged her up the steps and along the dock.

"That would be my first choice. But maritime law frowns on such practices today."

"What, then? Are you going to chain me up and make me your prisoner?"

"An appropriate description." He grasped her around the waist and hoisted her onto the deck. She landed on shaky legs, but managed to twist around to face him as he bounded aboard. He indicated the entrance with a jerk of his head.

She balked. "An appropriate description of what?" This time her voice hadn't been nearly so self-assured.

The anger in his eyes made her shiver with foreboding. "What do you intend to do with me?"

He eyed her levelly, his rage evident in the flare of his nostrils. "What the hell do you think I'm going to do with you?"

She shook her head, bewildered. One idea nagged, but she rejected it. Back there he'd pretended to be married to her. All those strangers, plus Grandpa and Aunt Jo, thought they were newlyweds. But surely he didn't intend to keep up that pretense. There was no reason why he should. She'd have thought he'd be delighted to expose her as the embezzler's granddaughter he thought she was. "I—I don't have any idea what you're going to do," she admitted faintly.

"For the next week, *darling*," he said, his voice hard, "we're going to be a happily married, honeymooning couple."

Her heart flip-flopped as he confirmed her worst fear. "No..."

The grin he flashed was devilish, but devoid of humor. "Oh, yes." Shocking her to her core, he lifted her into his arms and carried her down a short hallway. Before them, the master suite door stood ajar. He didn't even slow down when he got to the room's entrance, merely kicked open the barrier with a thundering bang, and stalked inside.

She gasped in fear when he tossed her on the bed. "What do you think you're doing?" Scrambling away from him, she hopped to the carpeted floor on the opposite side. "There are laws against rape, you know!"

He snorted derisively. "I love you, too, darling. But for the record, I'm not doing this out of any craving for your body or a desire to join the ranks of married men—far from it." He turned around and headed for the door, but before he left her, he peered back and gave her that same half grin that she'd found so devastating, yet lacking any warmth. "You fell into my lap—so to speak—at precisely the right moment, Ms. Stewart. Just so you'll fully understand my position, my company is family held, which means only relatives have voting stock. At least up until now. I have the most stock, naturally, since my grandfather started the company—"

"Yours and *mine!*" she interrupted, contempt ripe in her tone.

His half grin faded. "Nevertheless, once Kennard died, the bulk of the stock came to me. I suppose you've heard rumors about what a playboy I am."

She sniffed disdainfully. "You're too kind to yourself. Lecherous womanizer would be more appropriate!"

"Exactly my point, my rather unscrupulous reputation with women, plus petty jealousy over my inherited position in the company, has built up a smoldering resentment toward me from a certain faction of my board of directors. Though I've kept them in caviar and diamonds, that envious faction is crying conservatism, insisting I don't know the meaning of the word, and rabble-rousing to get me out as Chief Executive Officer. Their fear tactics have garnered almost enough votes to succeed. But," he added, eyeing her narrowly, flinty determination edging his words, "if they all believe I've settled down with a wife, I might have a chance to swing the votes in my direction and save Panther Automotive from disaster under the management of that maneuvering yes-man, Clayton Stringman."

"You—you mean you're going to pretend we're married just so you can keep control over—over...." She couldn't finish, stunned by the very idea. "And you call *me* a conniving liar?"

"Millions of dollars and thousands of jobs rest on the board's vote. I won't allow a handful of jealous, over-cautious cousins to throw all that away," he growled. *"Of course,* I'd pretend to be happily married to protect my company and my employees, Ms. Stewart. Don't be naive." He paused, his expression stony, then reminded, "If you'll think back, you begged me to go along with this fabrication."

She gulped at the fierce gleam in his eyes and the irate set of his jaw. "But that was only for a few *hours!"*

"You made your bed, Ms. Stewart. Nobody said there wouldn't be lumps."

Several tension-filled seconds passed before she found the nerve to protest. "I won't allow you to do this. It's—it's immoral!"

"It may be," he admitted, his tone grave. "But, remember your grandfather's frail health."

"He's leaving tonight," she reminded him haughtily.

"Not after I issue an invitation for him to remain the entire week." He turned to go, warning, "I hope you can play a blushing bride, Ms. Stewart."

"You wouldn't!" she shot back, but it was too late. As the slamming of the door echoed in her ears, it became horribly clear that Damon DeMorney was unscrupulous enough to do just that.

SHE WAS PACING when the door exploded open and Damon burst in.

Whirling to face him, she threw her arms akimbo. "What a charming way you have of entering rooms. Where did you learn it, executive commando camp?" It wasn't until then that she noticed his arms were filled with bags and boxes and women's clothes. "What in the world—"

"You have an hour to be ready for the party," he cut in.

"What party?" A wave of panic began to build inside her again. It was one thing to pretend to be his bride shut up, all alone, on his yacht, but quite another to live such a huge lie out in public.

He dumped the colorful froth of materials and boxes onto the bed and gave her a speculative look. "There's a formal cocktail party tonight. Originally it was to welcome the board members to my home, here. But Aunt Jo insists that since she missed our wedding, it must be in our honor."

Mercy pulled her lips between her teeth, upset by this latest bad news. "And, I suppose, since it fits into your plan to appear all married and settled and newly conservative, you went along with it wearing a big grin?"

He crossed his arms before his chest regarding her with hooded eyes. "Something like that."

"Well—what if I refuse?"

"You won't," he cautioned. "*Grandpa* is taking a nap so that he'll feel up to seeing your radiant face tonight."

Defeat coursed through her. She seemed to be trapped by her own ill-considered lie. Shifting uncomfortably, she looked away, mumbling, "How could Josephine swallow this wedding story? She introduced us less than four days ago on the yacht. When would we have had time to get married?"

He shrugged indolently. "You know her. Aunt Jo lives in her own little reality. Once she'd spoken with Otis, and he'd told her we'd been married for several weeks, she simply scolded me for playing such a trick on her." His brows contracted in a mild frown. "She assumes we met in Miami at some restaurant or theater, and fell madly in love. She's decided that our so-called act on the yacht was perpetrated so that we could announce our marriage down here."

"That's crazy," she said, appalled.

"Nevertheless, it's the story she's been content to pass along to anyone who will stand still long enough to listen."

She shook her head. "I can't believe this."

"Believe it, Ms. Stewart," he warned gravely. "But it's not the end of the world. After this board meeting ends and your grandfather goes back to the home, we'll wait a few weeks then say we got a quiet divorce. No one will be the wiser."

"I suppose…" It seemed like an awful lot of lying, but he was right. That would be the least problematic way to get out of this predicament. Her gaze dropped listlessly to the clothes on the bed. She'd forgotten about them. "Whose are these?" she asked without much interest.

"A local boutique delivered several cocktail dresses for your approval. What you don't want will be returned."

"I don't want any of them," she said glumly. "I'll wear my own clothes."

His humorless chuckle drew her glower. "Ms. Stewart," he began, directing a cool gaze her way. "How many evening gowns did you bring on this cruise?" He scanned her shorts-clad form dispassionately. "I don't intend to argue the point. Even if I did, there isn't time. You'll wear one of these."

His condescension irritated her, but she tried to compose herself. He was right about one thing. She didn't have any formals in her locker downstairs. Actually, she only had one dress on board and it was more suited for church than a cocktail party. With a resigned sigh, she walked to the bed and stared down at the jumble of fabric and boxes. "Okay, just go away. I'll be ready in an hour."

"My clothes are here. There's another bathroom. That can be yours."

She wasn't sure she'd heard right. Twisting around, she gaped at him. "You don't expect us to share this room while we change clothes?"

He'd opened a closet door and was retrieving a tuxedo. "Unfortunately, there will be servants coming and going on the yacht from time to time, not to mention Josephine's eccentric behavior. If we're to make this ruse believable, we're going to have to share this bedroom." Her jaw dropped in indignation as he calmly went on. "I'll sleep on the settee, if that's what's bothering you. As far as the bathroom goes, it's quite large and has everything you could need. I won't disturb you in there."

"How gallant!"

When he'd retrieved his clothes, he eyed her, and for a fleeting second she thought she saw amusement flicker in his glance. "I'll be as gallant as your lie, and my corporate problems, allow me to be. Is that clear enough—my love?'' He turned away and entered his bathroom. The door clicked shut at his back, leaving Mercy to gawk incredulously after him.

An hour later she was staring at herself in her floor-length bathroom mirror. She'd never worn expensive clothes before, and was in awe of the feel of the silk slip dress she'd decided on. It was like being draped in a gossamer scarf—all over. So airily soft, so—nothingness. The black silk was actually more of a lining for the delicate black lace outer layer. She felt like there should be another entire layer—possibly a turtleneck, long-sleeve, floor-length tweed suit. But, no. Apparently this skimpy attire was what fast-track people thought of as outerwear.

She scanned herself from her threadlike straps and modest show of cleavage on down along the curvy dress to a hem that seemed obscenely short, exposing as much thigh as her uniform shorts had. There had been a pair of sheer, black hose and a garter belt in with the jumble of things, and she'd slipped them on. She'd forgotten to bring any shoe boxes into the bathroom, so she had no idea what she'd end up wearing on her feet.

She inspected her dark blond hair. Defiantly, she'd opted to wear it as she always did, pulled back in a French twist at her nape. Wispy bangs fell into blue eyes that were now wider than usual in fearful anticipation. Several unruly wisps hung loose before her ears, and she couldn't decide if she was happy about that or not. Just how unruly did the smart set allow their hair to be? She touched a loose strand, trying to decide if she should smooth it into place or not. Finally, irritated that she'd even momentarily cared, she left it dangling. Maybe she had to pretend to be Damon DeMorney's bride, but it wasn't her duty, *or her desire,* to please him!

When she opened her bathroom door she was startled to see Damon standing on the opposite side of the bed, tying his black tie. He looked arrestingly elegant in his tuxedo jacket and slacks, and her breath caught in her throat. He glanced her way, his hawklike features serious. With an almost imperceptible squint of his eyes and a sideways movement in his jaw, he observed her for several heartbeats.

She tensed, feeling like a cornered animal in a hunter's crosshairs. He disapproved of what he saw! She was too skinny, too plain, her hair was too frumpy. Everything must be totally wrong, for his expression seemed troubled. She pinched her lower lip with her teeth, trying to prepare for his critical outburst.

After another second his eyebrows rose a trifle and he went back to tying his tie. "You're on time," he murmured.

She was more than a little startled by his minimal comment. "I—well, except for shoes." She busied herself rummaging through the boxes and uncovered a pair of black pumps, hurriedly slipping them on her feet. To her surprise, they fit. When she looked at Damon again, he was watching her, his expression unreadable.

With a nervous shiver she couldn't explain, she glanced away. "I'm ready."

"Why aren't you wearing any jewelry?"

She blanched, going defensive. "I foolishly allowed Queen Elizabeth to borrow my diamond tiara."

His contemptuous frown made it clear he wasn't in the mood for sarcasm. Without comment, he bent to the bed and began to riffle through the mound of discarded dresses. Mercy watched him, unable to keep herself from scanning his white-blond hair and strong profile. Her gaze slid from the crisp, white collar of his formal shirt and black tie, across broad shoulders encased in expensive black silk, to the white rosebud boutonniere in the lapel.

She even admired the precise correctness of his French cuffs protruding from his jacket sleeves, and the square, golden cuff links that sparkled and flickered in the light. He looked so stylish and cultivated. Even his black shoes glimmered with a million-dollar sheen. *He looks just like a bridegroom!* her mind wailed.

The magnitude of her lie hadn't really hit her until this second. She was going to have to convince not only her grandfather, but a whole lot of very savvy people that Damon DeMorney had actually picked *her* to be his life's partner. Unconsciously she touched her hair, wishing she'd taken more care with it. She was sure to look like a country bumpkin on his arm. She was petrified that even her ailing grandfather would see through their deceit once he saw them together tonight.

He straightened, coming up with a black velvet case. Opening it, he scanned the contents for a moment before extracting something small and sparkly. Snapping the case shut, he tossed it back on the bed and came over to her.

When she took a safeguarding step away, his expression grew rankled. "I'm not going to strangle you, Ms. Stewart," he assured her tiredly. "Stand still."

She saw that he was holding a pair of earrings, dainty yet exquisite. Each one had an inch-long strand of diamonds dangling from one larger round diamond that she guessed to be at least two carats in weight. "Are these—real?" she breathed as he attached them to her earlobes.

"Why, are you planning to steal them?"

His fingers were a warm contrast to his cold tone. She shot him a thoroughly annoyed look. "You know, I could grow to loathe you!"

He lifted his hands away from her face. A crooked smile touched one corner of his mouth as he drew something from his pocket. "Give me your left hand," he commanded quietly, taking her fingers in his without waiting for her to comply. Before she realized what he was doing, he'd slipped a pair of rings on her finger. The first was a simple golden wedding band, the second, a fabulous square-shaped diamond. "Loathe me all you please in private, Ms. Stewart," he said as he released her. "But in front of my board of directors I expect you to be convincingly adoring."

As she stared at the wedding set sparkling from her left hand an unanticipated sadness enveloped her heart. Every woman wanted this—a wedding ring. But she'd gotten hers from a man she'd just told she could easily loathe, and he'd only grinned at her, insisting he didn't care. It was all such an ugly sham. If it weren't for her grandfather's delicate health, she would snatch the costly rings from her finger and fling them in his insolent face. But she couldn't do that, and she knew she couldn't—and what was worse, Damon DeMorney *knew* she knew it.

She was drained; her heart wasn't into arguing anymore, and she shrugged. "I'll pretend to adore you in public," she promised through a dejected sigh. As she faced him again, she was surprised that he was blurred by unhappy tears. Fighting them back, she forced a tight smile, whispering thinly, "But in private, you and I will know the truth, won't we—*darling*."

THE EVENING was passing in a strained haze for Mercy. Damon's home was spread out over a large area, and she hesitated venturing too far from the great room, for fear she'd get lost in the tangle of hallways never to be seen again.

As she plastered on a smile and tried to listen to the small talk of several bejeweled corporate wives, she had to admit that Damon's island hideaway was an open, airy treasure. There were multitudes of skylights and picture windows well suited to the many tropical plants and flowers that filled and enlivened the place. Right now, a bright moon and a thousand pinprick stars could be seen above her head, so lovely and peaceful over the drone of conversation.

As she nodded, half listening to a discussion about fashion trends, she let her gaze and her mind cruise. The low, sleek furniture, cushioned with slubbed white cotton, looked as though it, too, had been part of the architectural design. The house was an eloquent composition of bold lines and angles, its stucco and rough beams all painted a monochromatic white, while the floors were irregular slabs of shiny black slate, a vibrant counterpoint to the light tones of the rest of the dwelling.

Shimmering works of modern art gave drama to stark walls. Adding additional touches of texture and color, were tasteful black marble carvings, Byzantine stone bowls, Italian wrought-iron candelabra and rustic copper planters. It was all so formidable and splendid, yet there was a chill about the place—like a museum rarely visited, dusted yet neglected in some basic way.

This was no home for Damon, no haven. There wasn't a single family photograph, no trite yet lovable mementos, no signs of warmth or affection anywhere. She wondered about his parents, who they had been and why they'd lived here—and why their son had not?

Mercy's glance fell on the chunky Santa Claus of a man named Clayton Stringman, Damon's business antagonist. He was standing beside his thin, pinch-faced wife among a group of several other couples. Clayton, appearing to be in his early fifties, looked quite lovable. His chuckle was infectious, and even his cheeks were the deep pink of a jolly old elf.

Yet after he'd come over and hugged her for the fourth time, Mercy began to think he was either being exploitively doting or he was very forgetful. She wondered if Damon might have had a point about the man being manipulative. In her opinion, he might also be half-witted. She hated to admit there was anything about the older man that bothered her. After all, *she* was on Clayton's side and hoped he'd take over the reins of the company.

But poor Clayton was certainly running a pale second tonight. This party was on Damon's turf, and it was his evening to charm the board. He'd left her about ten minutes ago to "work the room," as he'd put it. Now he was being Mr. Charisma. Mr. Accessible. Mr. Settled-Down-Conservative. How he did all three so well, she couldn't imagine.

She'd never seen corporate politics in action, but she felt tension crackle in the air between the Stringman faction and the DeMorney camp. She now could see, first-hand, that she was a throwaway pawn in a multimillion-dollar power struggle, and was way out of her league.

She didn't know the rules for playing the cutthroat game, Survival of the Richest, but Damon obviously did. She'd watched him as he'd moved among his guests, laughing and talking. There was a striking, confident quality in him that people were attracted to. Yet, when necessary, he could emanate a charmingly believable humility. She had to give credit where credit was due. Behind that captivating facade was a brilliant, hard-nosed strategist who knew what he wanted and planned to have it.

She caught sight of him by chance. Or was it really all that much by chance, since he stood a head taller than every other man in the room? He was conversing with that attractive woman she'd seen him with several times. What was her name? Buffy Something. She only knew the woman was the widow of one of Damon's cousins, and now controlled his voting stock. Watching Damon grin at the woman, Mercy could tell he was working her—whether it was for votes or something more carnal, she couldn't be sure.

Buffy looked to be in her early thirties, and had the sort of well-rounded figure that readers of *Playboy* magazine would appreciate. Tonight she was hiding none of her assets in a red, crushed-velvet bustier and long, skinny black skirt that sported a slit all the way to her hip. She had a boyish haircut that came as close to the color of Damon's hair as a bottle of peroxide could provide.

She grimaced to herself. *What a catty thing to think!* What did it matter to her if this Buffy person was standing there stark naked, completely bald and doing a bump-and-grind seduction in front of Damon? It was of no interest to her at all!

She felt pain, and realized she was clutching her hands in a ball, her nails digging into her flesh. Deciding she needed to do something, keep busy and take her mind off this whole, awful fraud, she excused herself from the cluster of wives, mumbling something about getting a glass of sea grape punch.

As she maneuvered her way toward the far-off dining room, she became more conscious of the music from the small, hired band that drifted over the low rumble of conversations. There was a definite island lilt to the tunes they played, though the melodies were familiar. "Yesterday" by the Beatles had just begun and, as usual, she heard a quaint reggae beat to it that hadn't been in the original recording.

"I think we should dance," came a voice at her back.

She shifted her head to see Damon smiling down at her. His loving expression startled her and did strange unbidden things to her insides. Before she had time to respond, he took her by the hand to lead her to the center of the room where a few other couples had begun to sway to the plaintive strains of the rock and roll classic.

He drew her against him, his hand warm at her back. "Loosen up, darling. We're supposed to be in love." He smiled down at her. "You're as tense as a Victorian virgin on her wedding night."

She stumbled to a halt, dazed by his bluntness. "I—I beg your pardon?"

He bent to whisper near her ear. "We're supposed to be hot for each other." He nipped at her earlobe for the benefit of onlookers, and Mercy's knees went watery. Luckily he was holding her, so she managed to remain standing. "Bat your eyes. Giggle," he urged, his breath tickling her nape. "You know—like foreplay."

The blood drained from her face and she couldn't seem to help herself from stiffening further.

He straightened, studying her openly for a moment. "You're *not,* are you?"

"Not what?" she asked, oddly breathless.

One brow rose as though in skepticism. "A vir—"

"That's none of your business," she interrupted, her voice rising several octaves, even in a whisper. Aware that her sharp retort was practically an admission that she *was,* she hurriedly bluffed, "But—naturally, I'm *not!*" His torso, pressing against her breasts, was too warm, too male, for her peace of mind. Still she tried to smile seductively, even fluttered her lashes, insisting, "*Really,* I'm not."

He was moving her about the floor in a slow, sensuous dance, their bodies molded together like the most devoted lovers might be. His aroma filled her senses, so mellow, warm and woodsy. His fingers splayed out against the small of her back, another disconcerting area of scintillating warmth she was having trouble dealing with.

He said nothing for a long moment, nodded to someone who'd made a passing comment. She relaxed a bit, grateful that his upsetting cross-examination was successfully past.

Out of the corner of her eye she could see her grandfather sitting next to Josephine on a small couch. He looked as out of place in his rented tux as she felt in her borrowed dress, yet he seemed happy, and his color was good. She was grateful for that, at least.

Josephine was wearing another warm-up suit, her only concession to the fact that this was a formal occasion was that it was made of pink silk and her sandals glittered with rhinestones. She was also wearing a different wig. This one, a flowing platinum model, Mercy thought of as "The Dolly Parton."

Detecting movement, she noticed Aunt Jo was waving at her. Reinforcing her flagging smile, she waved back. Both Grandpa and Jo seemed so pleased by the match, she was sick at heart for what she was doing. She'd only meant her little lie to ease her grandfather's passing. If she'd had any idea it would all blow up the way it had, and spin so crazily out of control, she would *never* have lied in the first place.

Yet, caught as she was, unable to undo what she'd started, she had no choice but to try as hard as she could to loosen up, to press herself to Damon in an enticing manner, pretending they were a happy bride and groom.

With deep misgivings, she knew she must get back to gazing into his eyes. When she flicked her unwilling glance to his face, she had a shock. He was watching her, a corner of his mouth curved knowingly. *He knew she'd been lying about her sexual experience. She hadn't fooled him at all!* "I would never have guessed," he murmured, his vivid green eyes alight with taunting laughter, "from the way you kissed me."

She could barely manage to keep from squirming beneath his amused scrutiny. "I have no idea what you're talking about," she hedged through a faltering smile.

His deep chuckle tingled against her breasts, further shredding her already tattered nerves.

CHAPTER FIVE

THE PARTY had been stressful for Mercy. But with a shudder of dread, she realized it had been as easy as boiling water compared to what she was facing now.

Damon had made a big point of their leaving the party early—allowing everyone to believe the newlywed couple wanted to be alone. Since they weren't really newlyweds, and she, at least, had no earthly desire to be alone with him, she assumed he'd planned to get to bed because of early meetings in the morning. *At least that's what she hoped he'd planned.* For all she knew, with that playboy reputation of his, Damon might be planning a little leisure-time seduction of one particular captive virgin!

She stood inside her fancy yacht bathroom, clad in a red, oversize T-shirt she'd gotten upon graduation from the Culinary Institute of America. It had foot-high, black letters on the front that read C.I.A. Most people thought those initials stood for the well-known Central Intelligence Agency, a shadowy spy organization. Every time she wore the shirt, that misunderstanding got a laugh. Tonight, however, she wore it, not for laughs but because it was the largest thing she owned that she could sleep in. She tugged at the hem. Though it came almost to her knees, which was longer than her dress had been, she still felt vulnerable.

She'd managed to waste an hour in the bathroom, so it had to be midnight by now. Running a tired hand across her eyes, she faced the fact she couldn't cower in there forever. The head was big, but there were no comfortable places to sleep. Sooner or later she had to leave.

She finally decided the best plan would be to dash to the bed and quickly slip beneath the covers. Hopefully, Damon was asleep on the settee and wouldn't even be aware of her comings and goings. If he did happen to be awake, he'd see her for only a second or two before she was safely under the bedsheets and out of his amused sight.

With a quick intake of breath, she opened the door and dashed halfway to the bed before she registered the fact that the lights were on and Damon was nowhere to be seen. She glanced toward the door to his head. It stood ajar. "Mr. DeMorney?" she called, though not very loudly, for she wasn't sure she wanted to engage him in conversation, considering he might be, er, undressed.

There was no reply.

Puzzled, she walked around the bed to glance into his bathroom. All was quiet, and predictably neat. There was a lightweight terry robe on a golden hook beside the glassed-in shower. She frowned. It didn't appear he'd even begun to get ready for bed. Where could he have gone? When she'd scurried into her bathroom an hour ago, she'd been led to believe he was going straight into his to shower and then go to bed.

A quick, disobedient thought flitted through her brain, a vision of Damon stealing off to meet Buffy What's-

Her-Name in the moonlight, but she squelched it. That would be foolish of him, considering he was trying to prove to the board that he was a reformed, settled man. Still, hormones sometimes didn't listen to the logical brain. *She* was an excellent example of that, considering how, out on that dance floor tonight, she'd felt illogically drawn to Damon DeMorney. *Of all people!*

She closed her eyes, trying to blot out that uncomfortable memory. Well, hormones or no hormones, logic or no logic, she certainly wasn't going to trek off looking for him. If he wanted to take such a chance by meeting Busty Buffy, that was his business. As long as her grandfather didn't find out about the make-believe marriage, that was all she needed to worry about. Besides, the more damage Damon did to his chances at keeping control of his company, the happier she should be, shouldn't she?

Absently she turned off a lamp burning on a dresser beside Damon's bathroom door. That left only one wall sconce on, near the entry. Its glow was relatively dim, so she decided to leave it. Damon would have to see her in his bed, when and if he did show up. That way he couldn't crawl in beside her and later plead that he'd forgotten she was there. She might be a virgin, but she wasn't a dumb virgin.

Just as she reached for the bedspread, preparing to climb in, the door opened and Damon stalked in, looking irritated. "Get in!" he commanded in a rough whisper. He was jerking off his tie and making quick work of discarding his formal shirt, revealing a lightly furred, muscular chest. "Aunt Jo and Otis are coming."

Mercy had gone stark still in her bent-over position, staring as Damon stripped off his clothes and carelessly threw them about. He sat down on the bed and yanked off his shoes, tossing them aside. Next, the belt came off. Mercy gaped as it arced into the air and landed on the settee, only to slither off and drop soundlessly to the carpet.

She cast her gaze to the bedspread, afraid to look at him now. The only clothing he had left to remove were his tuxedo trousers, and she didn't intend to witness *that*. She felt a weight on the bed nearby. "Ms. Stewart, get in!" he ordered again, but barely above a whisper.

Unable to stop herself, she jerked to look at him. He was slipping beneath the covers, still clad in his formal slacks. As he settled in to lounge against the curved teak headboard, she heard a rap on the door. That small sound seemed to release her from her stupor, and she scurried beneath the covers.

"Come in," Damon called, and when she turned to glare at him, she found herself surrounded by strong arms hugging her beneath her breasts and pulling her against his chest. She managed to suppress a gasp only by sheer force of will.

"Surprise, surprise, children!" chirped Aunt Jo as she preceded Otis into the room, carrying two champagne glasses in each hand. She was flushed and smiling, her blond wig askew, but she didn't seem tipsy, just slightly out of breath.

"Happy wedding, Messy Miss and Damon, boy," Otis croaked, holding a bottle aloft. "We've come to toast the bride and groom in private."

"Hope we're not intruding," Jo added, hustling to the bed and holding out a hand for them to each take one of the glasses. "Oh, aren't you two the cutest couple," she cried. "Otis." She gestured for him to come closer. "I knew the minute I saw them together on the yacht they were in love." She tsk-tsked, shaking her head at them. "And you two thought you could fool me."

Mercy experienced a twinge of guilt. She wondered what Damon was thinking and was dying of curiosity to see his expression. She couldn't tell a thing from her position, with her back against his chest and his chin brushing the top of her head. She surmised his smile was as pained as hers.

Otis unscrewed the bottle lid and was pouring liquid into the glasses that she and Damon had taken from Jo. The drink was obviously not champagne, but something darker and thicker.

"What—what is that you're pouring, Grandpa?" she asked, trying to sound at ease.

"Something of Josephine's. She says it does wonders for the vitality."

"Asparagus tonic," the older woman trilled. "Part of my regime to regain my youthful constitution." She patted Otis's cheek. "And if I can be forthright, I must say your grandfather could benefit from some rejuvenating. He's just too pale." She lifted her glass, now filled with a gray-green liquid, and gushed, "To Damon and Mercy, our dear, dear children. May they give us beautiful babies—*soon!*" She smiled at them. When she focused on her grandnephew, her eyes filled with tears. "I'm so happy for you, Damon. I feared you would never marry, since you didn't have a very—well—close family life of your own. I tried to be like a mother to you, but I was afraid my efforts weren't enough."

Mercy could feel Damon stiffen and knew he was not happy by this turn of the conversation. Unaware of her grandnephew's tension, Josephine chattered on. "But I'm elated I was wrong! Well, here's to your happiness, you two!"

"Cheers," came Damon's deep voice. Mercy could detect a tightness in his tone. She shifted so she could watch him from the corner of her eye as he heartily drank. It amazed her that he was able to pretend so well. If she hadn't been in intimate contact with his rigid torso, she would have believed that he was a carefree bride-groom.

Both Jo and Otis downed their tonic immediately. Mercy toyed with hers, not because she dreaded the taste, for she didn't. Josephine had insisted she drink the stuff several times in the past weeks, saying young women needed to concern themselves with their vitality, too.

No, she hesitated because she could feel Damon's strong heartbeat, could detect his powerful maleness through the thin cotton of her T-shirt. The idea of having this man make love to her—to be the mother of his children—well, the very thought sent a female tingling through her, and she wasn't happy about that feeling.

"Drink up, Messy Miss," Otis urged. "It's pretty tasty, if you ask me."

Hurriedly, Mercy drank her tonic, though the lump of anxiety in her throat made it difficult to swallow.

"Oh, before we leave you two lovebirds alone," Jo said, "I'd like to have that file of recipes you were cook-ing for me all month, Mercy, dear. I want Chef Charles to cook them for Otis and me while he's visiting."

"Oh," Mercy objected, handing her empty glass to her grandfather. "Please, Aunt Jo, let me cook for you and Grandpa. I'm sure Chef Charles will have his hands full with the other guests—"

"Nonsense," she scoffed. "Damon doesn't want you slaving away on your honeymoon! Besides, it won't hurt some of those cholesterol-riddled relatives of mine to get a taste of healthy food a time or two." She bent to brush a kiss first on Damon's cheek, then Mercy's. "Now enjoy yourselves. Otis and I will get that file and be on our way."

Mercy nodded apathetically, knowing she had little choice. "The file's in the bottom drawer to the left of the refrigerator."

"We'll be off, then." She tossed back a cheery wave. "Come, Otis, dear. The other thing I want to make sure of is that you get plenty of sleep. Rest, healthy food and happy thoughts. That's the ticket to vigorous corpuscles!"

Suddenly the elderly couple was gone and the room had fallen deadly still. Mercy started to wriggle out of Damon's hold, but he held her fast. "Wait a minute. Let's make sure they're gone."

Held captive in the circle of his arms, she couldn't recall experiencing such an eternal minute in her life. Everything she thought or felt or smelled seemed to be intensified a thousand times. She even began to imagine she could feel the masculine energy that made him so self-confident radiating from him.

Although his hands remained beneath her breasts, he didn't take liberties, didn't grope. Still she sensed a quickening inside her, a thrill at the contact, as though he'd touched her like a lover, and she was stirred by it.

He smelled good, too, very good, and she couldn't help but inhale deeply of him, getting sinful pleasure in the act. As she consciously breathed his fragrance in and out, in and out, his chest began to seem exactly the right size to snuggle against. She found herself doing just that and scanning the sheer, athletic beauty of his arms. She started to relax, luxuriating in what had been a forced closeness only minutes ago.

Somewhere in the back of her brain, she perceived a sound—possibly a door closing off in the distance—but it didn't quite register.

"They're gone," he murmured.

"Who?" she asked through a long sigh. She didn't really care, for she was savoring an odd, inner glow that was awfully nice. Why not simply float along on this toasty, thick cloud of contentment, and not allow herself to be disturbed?

Something began to intrude on her pleasure. She snuggled deeper, trying to dislodge whatever the disturbance was. But it kept on—the same tingly reverberation was running through her that she'd felt earlier that night on the dance floor.

Her eyes flew open when she became fully aware of the fact that Damon was *chuckling*. "I thought only babies and adults with a clear conscience could fall asleep that quickly," he teased. "Apparently that's not true."

She swallowed hard, having forgotten about Otis and Aunt Jo and the colossal lie that had forced them to be cuddled together like this. What was wrong with her?

She all but vaulted from his arms. "I wasn't asleep," she retorted, which was the truth. "I was merely playing the part of a loving bride." That, of course, was *not* the truth, but she couldn't tell him she'd found herself relishing their intimacy, wanting it to go on and on. Scrambling off the bed, she defended, "I thought—thought that's what you wanted. Now, will you kindly get out of *my* bed? Or did you lie about that, too?"

He'd propped himself up on his elbows and grinned at her. "I like the shirt."

She didn't know how to respond to his offhand comment, and didn't think shouting, *Why, you dirty-minded womanizer, how dare you!* would quite fit. Her mouth worked several times before she finally managed, "Thank you, Mr. DeMorney. Now, would you please get out of the bed?"

He lifted a doubtful brow. "Ms. Stewart, have I offended you in any way while we've shared this bed?"

His bluntness made heat creep up her face. "Why—er, I suppose not."

Sliding out from beneath the covers, he stood up, so tall, so gloriously male. When his glance fell on her face again, his eyes held an intense flicker. "Just remember this. The only time you need expect my advances is when you request them. I don't rape women—especially faint-hearted virgins."

Awkwardly she cleared her throat. "I keep telling you, I'm not—"

"Prove it," he challenged softly. He said nothing more, merely loomed there looking sexy and irresistible, with a skeptical half grin on his lips.

A shiver of willful excitement rushed through her. She was sure she must be a blazing crimson by now, and was humiliated and resentful that the man could affect her so thoroughly. "You—you think you're heaven's gift to sexual abandon, I suppose! Well, you're not, Mr. DeMorney!" she snapped. "Personally, I find you totally—completely..." She was at a loss for words. *What?* Nothing descriptive came to her mind, and she was further mortified to discover that his slow, knowing grin could short-circuit her brain.

By now, his expression was openly amused. With a quick flash of teeth, he gave her a nod. "Good night, darling." He pivoted away to disappear into his bathroom.

After he'd gone, she stood there fairly trembling with rage. What was her problem? Why couldn't she think of any curt, descriptive adjectives? Words like—egotistical, tedious, obtuse, overbearing! They were all wonderful descriptions that she would have loved to shout at him. But she hadn't been able to think of any until he'd ensconced himself inside his bathroom.

Irritated to the brink of insanity, she marched around the bed and banged on his bathroom door. "For your information, Mr. DeMorney, you're conceited, insensitive, tiresome—" *good, the words were spilling out now. Excellent, pithy words!* "—smart-mouthed, boorish—"

The door was flung open and Damon was suddenly there. She was struck speechless by the fact that he was naked except for a towel he'd tied about his waist. "Yes?" he queried, leaning casually against the doorjamb. "Did I hear you say something about wanting to prove something to me?"

She flinched at his taunt, stumbling a step away. *For heaven's sake, Mercy*, her mind cried. *Change the subject! Anything. Think of anything!* All of a sudden the wonderful, pithy words she'd been shouting at him through the door dissipated like an indistinct dream. She was at a loss for insults, again, darn the man! Deciding to take the offensive, she blurted, "I—I merely wanted to know—to know—*where you were tonight?*" Well, at least it was a change in subject, and maybe it would put Mr. Superior on *his* defensive for a change!

Damon's expression darkened slightly in confusion. "When?"

"Before Grandpa and Aunt Jo came here."

He pursed his lips, nodding in understanding. "I was working in my office on board, why?"

She didn't have any idea why she was asking, except maybe the Buffy thing was still lingering in the back of her mind. "What were you doing in there? I suppose it would be too much to hope you were ordering an audit or whatever you'd call it for when Grandpa was fired— to *prove* his innocence!"

His expression grew forbidding. "Get off that, Ms. Stewart. It's a pipe dream that can't possibly come true."

"Are you afraid to find out the truth?"

Straightening to his full height, he muttered an oath. "I don't have time for this. If you'll remember, my life isn't all roses right now, either." He cocked his head inquiringly. "While we're on the subject, how did you like Clayton Stringman?"

She was having trouble concentrating in the face of all his bare skin. As nonchalantly as she could, she shifted her gaze toward the marble tub to his left. "I thought he was charming," she muttered.

"Like hell, you did."

Shocked at his ability to read her mind, her gaze rocketed to his face. "Why would you say a thing like that?" she asked, purposely sidestepping his remark.

"Because I've gotten to know you, and you're a lousy liar. I could see in your expression tonight that you thought he was a shifty jerk."

She huffed disdainfully, spinning away, wishing she weren't so transparent to this man. "If you want the truth, I hope he beats the pants off you!"

"You mean *towel*, don't you?"

She swallowed, trying to suppress hot images of him losing that towel. Apparently her body language was quite entertaining, for once again she was forced to listen to his disturbing chuckle.

WHEN MERCY AWOKE the next morning, Damon was gone, all evidence that he'd slept on the settee removed. After an awkward breakfast in bed, served by a clearly curious but closedmouthed Bonnie, Mercy dressed in a pair of white slacks, red knit top and sandals, and emerged from the yacht as Mrs. Damon DeMorney.

She wanted to work up her nerve before she faced anyone, so she decided to sit on the beach and collect herself. But she found she wasn't alone long. The news spread quickly that Damon's young bride was out and about. Within minutes various cousins found her and engaged her in conversation. It was clear they were trying to pry information out of her, about how she and Damon had met, about Damon's future plans for the company, anything at all. She tried to smile while keeping her answers vague, for she knew nothing about almost everything they wanted to know.

During these disquieting chats, she managed to get more information than she gave, and found out that Kennard had had four sisters. All but Josephine, the baby of the family, had married and produced abundant offspring. Now all the offspring had stock in Panther Automotive, and most of them were afraid of Damon's bold management tactics.

She found out from little comments here and there that Damon's relatives were frightened of losing their diamonds and their summer homes and their expensive private-club memberships, if Damon made a strategic business mistake in today's shaky economy. She was startled by how many of the board members' wives came to her, appealing that she use her "influence" to convince Damon to pull back on one objective or rethink another agenda.

She was grateful when Josephine intervened and announced that Damon had insisted she take his bride on a shopping trip. Before leaving, however, Mercy checked on her grandfather, who'd decided to take a long nap. After kissing his pale cheek, she was whisked away in a sleek, chauffeured, black Excellenta, the largest and most luxurious of the Panther line.

Mercy enjoyed Jo's cheery attitude, and their afternoon in some of the most elegant shops in Georgetown unfolded like a fairy tale. She felt horrible guilt about the money she was spending in the guise of Mrs. Damon DeMorney, and kept asking, "Did Damon *really* insist on this?"

Josephine only laughed, adding yet another gown or pair of shoes or skimpy negligee to the swelling account, persisting that he had.

On the way home Jo giggled, drawing Mercy from reflections of her growing list of misdeeds. She hadn't been able to even calculate a dollar figure for what she'd purchased today and was filled with remorse. Josephine's unexpected tittering was so out of place in the dark hole where her mood had taken her, she almost shrieked.

"Dear, are you all right?" Jo touched her arm. "You nearly jumped through the sunroof."

Mercy faced the older woman and smiled feebly. "I'm fine. Did—did you think of something funny?" She knew she could use a good laugh.

Jo blushed all the way to her Cher wig roots. "Well, dear," she whispered, touching Mercy's hand. "I suppose I can tell you this now. You see, I'm just happier than I've been in years."

Mercy couldn't hold on to her smile any longer, for she sensed Jo's happiness had something to do with her lie. "Happy?" she echoed.

Jo nodded. "Oh, it was my deep, dark secret for a long time, and I was very ashamed of it for years."

Mercy blanched, unable to think of a thing to say. What deep, dark secret could this sweet, eccentric woman have?

"It's about your grandfather, Otis." She patted Mercy's hand, then took hold of her fingers, squeezing them as though she needed to for reassurance. "You see, years ago, when I came back from finishing school in New York, I met your grandfather. I was twenty-one and he was twenty-five, and married, with a baby daughter.

That darling child would have been your mother, of course." Jo's flush deepened. "Oh, this is just so embarrassing, but I feel I can tell you. You see, I fell deeply in love with Otis at my very first sight of him, but naturally he was off-limits, being a married man."

Mercy could tell her lips had opened in a soundless "oh" but even if she'd had anything to say, she didn't have the chance, for Jo was rushing on. "Oh, don't fret, dear, we didn't have an affair or anything so ugly as that. I simply loved him from afar for ten long years—until that awful day he left the company in—well—disgrace." She shook her head, sighing despondently. "I was heartbroken. I *never* believed Otis had a dishonest bone in his body. But Kennard was furious. Wouldn't listen to me. I was, after all, only a woman." She squeezed Mercy's hand again. "I knew I'd never see Otis again, and because of that I didn't speak to Kennard for years. Anyway, just—well what I'm trying to say is, I was hoping I'd have your support now."

Mercy frowned, perplexed. "My—my support?" Her throat was dry, and she cleared it. "Support for what?"

Jo giggled again, sounding like a nervous schoolgirl. "The truth is, I never fell out of love with Otis. And seeing him again, I was hoping—perhaps this might be my chance to—to find my own happiness, at last." She paused, her eyes filling with self-conscious tears. "And, naturally, I'd like to give that sweet man some happiness, too. Don't hate me for saying this, but I don't believe he's been happy for a long time." Her hold on Mercy's fingers became painful. "Do you think I have a chance with..." She stopped speaking to bite her lip. When a tear slid down that pudgy, rouged cheek, Mercy was so overcome with emotions she thought she might start crying, too.

Josephine DeMorney had been hopelessly in love with her grandfather for fifty years. She felt a nauseating, sinking gloom invade her soul. Her lie had now sucked in another innocent victim. Poor Josephine, getting her hopes raised again after all these years. She hated herself for putting this woman's heart and hopes at risk, too.

A lump blocking her throat, she took the woman into her arms. "Oh, Aunt Jo, I had no idea." Pulling slightly away, she looked into the woman's watery green eyes, the same lovely green as Damon's, and she smiled wanly. "Grandpa's a lucky man to have earned your affection. And he certainly could use a little happiness in his life." As the car pulled down the winding DeMorney drive, she hugged the older woman's shoulders. Hesitating, she hated to add a sad note, but after a few seconds she knew she was obliged to say this. "Of course, you know Grandpa's not in the best of health—"

"Dear me, I could tell immediately," Jo admitted. "That's why I've taken him under my wing. I intend to build him up, make him feel wanted and needed. You'll be surprised, dear, what my tender loving care will do."

Mercy nodded, working at keeping a brave face. She'd tried to contact Otis's doctor yesterday afternoon, but he'd been in surgery so she'd said she'd try later. Then the bottom had dropped out of her plans when Damon forced her into publicly being his bride. She hadn't even thought to call back. As soon as she could, though, Mercy planned to find out what he thought of all this, and if he'd approved this trip. Attempting to keep her fears out of her voice, she whispered, "I hope you're right, Aunt Jo. I—I want you to be right."

Josephine kissed Mercy's cheek and sat back with a relieved sigh, dabbing at her eyes with a handkerchief. "Well, I must compose myself, or what will Otis think of me?" She reached up to the front seat and tapped the driver's shoulder, calling loudly, *"Ebanks?"*

The young man, a Grand Cayman native, removed the headset from one ear so that his reggae music was no longer blaring directly into his brain. "Yes, Miss DeMorney, mum?" he inquired in a quaint accent reminiscent of an American Southern drawl mixed with a Scottish lilt.

"Ebanks, the young Mrs. DeMorney is running late for the beach cookout, so stay with her and carry the things she needs to the yacht, please."

"Yes, mum." He nodded as he pulled to a halt on the circle drive before the house.

"What beach cookout?" Mercy asked. This was the first she'd heard of it.

Josephine blew delicately into a handkerchief, then deposited the lacy bit of pink linen in her purse. "Oh, didn't I mention it? Now, you run back to the yacht and get into one of those delicious bathing suits you bought. Damon is probably already there since it's after six." She made a rather sour face. "I told Chef Charles to use your recipes for tonight's cookout, but he had a fit, raging he'd already made nearly all of the delicacies for the party and he would abandon us forever if I forced the issue." She shrugged. "Silly man was near tears, so I fear dinner tonight will be decadent." She smiled slyly. "Otis and I, of course, will have to dine alone on healthy salads and asparagus tonic. When I must, I can whip up a pretty tasty meal.''

Mercy noticed that the idea of being alone with Otis had caused a girlish sparkle to spring to life in Jo's eyes, and she was touched by it. But her mind kept turning back to what she'd said earlier—about Damon already being on the yacht getting ready for the *party*. She didn't relish the idea of another public function where she'd have to pretend to be his adoring bride again, so soon— especially clad only in skimpy swimming attire.

She noticed the young chauffeur, who'd finally relinquished his headphones, was helping Josephine out of the car. "Oh, Mercy, dear," Jo added, reaching back to fondly touch the younger woman's hand. "I keep forgetting to say this, but I know you'll make Damon very happy."

Mercy bit the inside of her cheek, thinking forlornly, *Only if I walk into the ocean and keep on going!*

CHAPTER SIX

DAMON WASN'T ON the yacht when Mercy arrived, after all. Ebanks helped her with her bundles and then left her alone. As she stood in the stillness of the huge master suite she was at a loss, wondering whether or not to get ready for the party. Jo hadn't mentioned a specific time, and she'd been in such a state of shock over the older woman's admission of love for her grandfather, she hadn't thought to ask.

She decided she'd walk back to the main house and ask somebody, but when she reached the foyer and had partly opened the door that led to the deck, she stopped in her tracks. Damon was coming along the dock, his expression closed and contemplative. She watched his approach in something like a trance. It struck her anew every time she saw him, how physically magnificent he was, and today was no exception.

He was wearing a white, drop-shoulder shirt that accented the astounding width of his shoulders. His black belt and white, pleated trousers with their relaxed fit, served to highlight his trim waist. All in all, he was the picture of casual good taste, looking crisp, yet comfortable, his platinum hair glistening in the late-afternoon sun like new snow. Mercy felt her heart turn over, convinced she would never see a more erotic sight under any tropical sun if she searched for the rest of her natural life.

She scanned his features, unable to tell from his expression if he was upset or just deep in thought, and she wondered how his day had gone. It shocked her that she even registered such a thought. *She didn't care a twit about his day!*

When he bounded aboard, he swept the door open, finding himself unexpectedly chest to nose with her. He halted abruptly, his features exhibiting surprise then closing in displeasure. "Ms. Stewart, lurking behind doors can be dangerous, unless you want to be run down."

She blushed, not aware that she'd let go of the door and had been standing dumbly behind it, thinking about *him,* of all people in the world to dwell on. Feeling both restless and peevish, and unsure why, she retorted, "Well, if you'd ever *tell* me what's happening, I might not have to keep going in search of information! I didn't know anything about this party tonight until Jo mentioned it. I was on my way to find out when I had to be ready just as you burst in!"

A shadow of annoyance crossed his face, but Mercy had the feeling he was more annoyed with himself than with her. He plunged his hands into his slash pockets, and exhaled tiredly. "Forgive me, Ms. Stewart, I thought Jo would remember to tell you. It starts at eight o'clock. I'll be occupied with business for several hours. You go on without me."

"Aren't you coming?" she asked, startling herself with the question.

He'd half turned, heading toward his office. With a tired shrug, he glanced down at her. "I'll join the party when I have time. I'm still running a company, you know."

She frowned, not looking forward to facing his nosy, self-centered relatives alone. "I'll wait for you," she murmured.

A brow lifted in what appeared to be surprise, but she didn't suppose he could be more surprised than she, for she'd had no idea she was going to say that until it came out of her mouth. "You'll wait for me?" he repeated. "Why in hell would you want to do that?"

She cast her gaze away, uncomfortable. "Grandpa and Jo won't be there. I don't know those people. All they want to do is grill me about my past, my grandfather, and insist I use my influence on you."

"Use your influence on me?" His wry tone irritated her, and she couldn't understand why. "Do you mean they expect you to influence me with pillow talk, Ms. Stewart—that they expect you to climb naked into my arms, make love to me and between gasps of pleasure coax me to become more conservative in my business dealings?"

The sexy picture he painted stunned her, siphoning the blood from her face, and she took in a sharp breath.

He chuckled morosely. "Don't tell me you thought all business decisions were made in the board room."

She couldn't find her voice, could only stare, wide-eyed.

His gaze grew circumspect, and he searched her pale face. "For all your lying and conniving, Ms. Stewart, sometimes you amaze me with your gullibility." He clenched his teeth, eyeing heaven. "What the hell," he acquiesced, sounding put out with himself. It was obvious he had enough troubles without concerning himself with hers, but for some reason he'd decided to take them into consideration. "Wait for me if you'd rather. My relatives can assume we're late because you've been—influencing me."

She stood there, upset and shaken, long after he'd disappeared into his office. For some demented reason she was unable to erase the image of their bodies entwined in passion, his kisses arousing her to gasps of pleasure....

MERCY'S MOOD was solemn as she secretly watched the party get under way from behind a tinted window in the main salon. Once again, she'd tried to reach Otis's doctor, but this time she was informed that he was out of town. She'd left her name and Damon's Grand Cayman number, but was frustrated at her continued failure to get any information. It seemed as though she was thwarted at every turn lately.

Deciding it would do no good to wallow in her troubles, she focused her attention on the party. Lights she didn't even know existed had blinked on high in the boughs of the trees that lined the beach, giving off a romantic glow over the sumptuous spread laid out on long tables. Pristine tablecloths were spread along the twenty-foot length of the buffet tables, covered with all manner of tropical fruits, flowers, and delicious-looking dishes Mercy could only guess at from this distance.

A reggae band was set up in the sand off to one side. People were wading, dancing, snorkeling and eating. Laughter abounded. Clayton Stringman was easy to spot in his pink Bermuda shorts, purple shirt, black knee socks and sandals. Ever since he'd arrived, some twenty minutes earlier, he'd been circulating among the party-goers. She realized he was "working" the group for all he could while Damon was away.

Following his rotund figure with her eyes, she watched as he hugged, guffawed, patted and kissed. Though she was wishing him luck, some small voice inside her was suggesting that it was deceitful of him to discredit Damon behind his back, while still managing to stuff down as much of his food as possible while doing it. She tried to force that negative idea back, telling herself this was big business, and evidently there were no rules requiring fair play.

"Ready to go?"

Mercy spun around, not having heard Damon's approach. He'd changed and was now clad in an aqua cotton shirt. Though it had buttons down the front, he'd left it open, exposing a wide strip of sinewy chest and washboard-taut belly. His swim trunks were a striking spatter-print design of aqua, yellow and navy. He wasn't wearing shoes, which explained why he'd managed to come up on her so quietly.

As he lounged against the salon door, his gaze roved over her in lazy appraisal. She felt a tremor along her spine, sure he would find her wanting. He was accustomed to polished society types. What must he think of her—a common sparrow pretending to be a peacock?

She'd never worn such an expensive swimsuit in her life. Even though this rose-colored design was a one-piece tank with no great show of either cleavage, hip or thigh, she felt underdressed. It had come with an ankle-length scarf skirt in swirls of pastels that could hardly be considered much in the way of clothes, for it was nearly transparent and opened all the way up her side to her waist, where it was tied. Though this swimsuit had been one of the least costly, and least skimpy, she still felt exposed beneath his scrutiny.

His gaze traveled back to her face, and then to her hair. She'd left it down, flowing just past her shoulders. She lifted her chin proudly. Let him find fault. It was fine with her if she didn't go to the party at all.

He grinned, startling her. "Come here," he said softly.

She blinked, half afraid to. What did he intend to do? When she hesitated for several more seconds, he crossed the distance between them and took her by the hand. "I'm not going to bite you, Ms. Stewart. Come on."

He led her to their suite and before she could protest he'd taken a sprig of brilliant yellow jasmine from a vase and turned to her. Surprising her further, he lifted the hair from her temple and held the flower there, scanning it as though trying to decide how it would look.

"What are you doing?" she asked, experiencing an odd stirring at his touch.

"Wear this in your hair tonight."

She nodded absently, her whole attention focused on the brush of his hand against her face. "I—I'll go pin them in."

When she took the sprig of flowers from him, she thought for a second his fingers lingered on hers, but decided she must be wrong. In her bathroom, she glanced at her face while she shakily fastened the flowers in her hair. Her cheeks were so flushed anyone would have thought she had a raging fever, or possibly just risen from a glorious round of honeymoon lovemaking. That thought made her blush deepen. She splashed her face with cold water and patted her skin dry before she re-emerged from the head. He was waiting for her by the door, his expression unreadable.

When she reached him, he entwined his fingers with hers. She glanced at him, confused. They weren't within sight of anyone, so there had been no need for the deception. Why had he taken her hand?

His expression closed, drawn in a frown, and he seemed to be light-years away in his mind. She grew peculiarly despondent about that. Somehow she'd sensed that when he'd given her the flowers there had been actual fondness in his glance. She shook herself of the thought. She didn't want him to be fond of her. She was *not* fond of him! No doubt he'd taken her hand merely to hurry her along.

An hour later Mercy had sampled so much delicious food she thought she'd never be able to eat again. The baked crab had been heavenly, as well as the roast yams, grape aspic, avocado salad and almond pie. She hadn't been able to bring herself to try either the turtle burgers or fried bolter, which was a specie of banana, sliced thin and fried. But it was just as well, for she knew she would explode with one more bite of anything.

Damon's arm had been gently encircling her waist most of the evening, yet she was still highly disconcerted by the warmth of his touch. Not because she didn't like it, on the contrary, she did, and that worried her terribly. Every so often, he reminded, "Put your arm around me," and she'd tentatively done so, but she felt like such a fraud.

They were wading in ankle-deep water. A sultry breeze ruffled her skirt, and the hem dipped and dived into the lapping waves, wetting it. Damon's arm, as usual, was wound about her, his large hand nearly encompassing her waist. She'd managed to work up her nerve to circle his waist with her arm. Unfortunately for her peace of mind, the frolicking breeze had lifted his shirt just as she'd slid her arm about him, so she was forced to cling to his bare skin, and was having a hard time thinking of anything else.

The music was low and erotic, the beat torrid and tropical, in the background. The stars twinkled above, winking at her, telling her they knew her predicament and found it intensely funny. It was too bad she didn't agree.

"You're very quiet," Damon said, surprising her from her unsettled musings.

She glanced up into his face. He was smiling at her, and that was so disconcerting she couldn't maintain eye contact. Casting her gaze out to the midnight-black sea, she whispered, "I hate what we're doing."

"You hate walking on a beach in the moonlight?"

She gave him a hostile, sidelong glance. "You know exactly what I mean. I don't understand how you can look so at ease. Or is lying through a smile a *major* part of big business?"

"I would remind you just whose lie this is, darling," he began, kissing her temple, "but your grandfather's coming."

She stiffened. "How do you know? We're facing the wrong way."

"Listen."

She stilled, straining to hear. After another second she heard him calling over the other laughing and chattering voices. "Messy Miss!" It was a gravelly, winded sound, but clearly her grandfather's voice. Releasing Damon's waist, she consciously rubbed her temple where she could still feel the tingle of his lips against her skin. Pivoting to face Otis, she faked a smile that had to be her poorest effort so far. "Hi, Grandpa. What is it?"

He was leaning on his cane, shuffling barefoot through the white sand, his slacks rolled up to reveal spindly ankles. A pig trotted along on each side of him, looking perfectly contented. When he reached them, he grinned broadly, first kissing Mercy's cheek, then hugging Damon. "I'm sorry I haven't been able—to visit with you two—today," he apologized, taking deep breaths between words. "But Josephine's been making me take it easy." He reached into his slacks' pocket and drew something out. "But—I wanted to get this to you, my boy—before I forgot."

Damon frowned when Otis held out his fist. "Here. This is yours."

Holding out a hand, Damon allowed the older man to drop something into his palm. "Found these between the cushions of the couch—in my room this morning. Would have weighed heavy on my conscience if I'd forgotten to get them to you."

When he'd drawn back his gnarled fist, Mercy stared down at what he'd given Damon. Four silver coins twinkled dully with reflected light. Otis was grinning at his granddaughter now. "Well, I'd best get back. Josephine's helping Chef Charles make your yogurt tarts, and I'm worried that she'll have him in tears if I don't hurry."

He turned away, made a smooching sound, calling, "Come along, Desi, Lucy. Dessert in a few minutes."

As he hobbled off, the pigs grunted their farewells and headed after him. Mercy shifted toward Damon as he watched her grandfather weave his way through guests lounging in chairs or on towels along the beach.

She sighed. "That's the man you think embezzled from your company?"

He glanced sharply at her, then down at the coins in his hand. Without comment, he slid the money into his swimsuit pocket. Taking her hand, he turned her away from the general crowd and led her off into deeper shadows.

"Where are we going?"

"Nowhere, just walking."

"Don't you have to work the room?"

He peered at her. "You learn fast." Glancing away, down the long strip of white sand before them, he shook his head. "I am working the room, Ms. Stewart. Remember, I'm supposed to be married, settled. It's expected that I'd want to walk off down the dark beach to be alone with my new bride."

She laughed out loud, but it was a pitiful sound, for she was laughing at herself for forgetting how shrewd this man was. Every move he made was orchestrated to enhance his position with his board of directors. Why did she have to lose sight of that every few minutes? Why did she have to have these foolish feminine flashes when she thought of him as merely a man and herself as merely a woman—strolling hand in hand under a tropical moon?

"Why the laugh?" he asked.

She ran a hand through her hair. "Nothing," she lied through a dispirited sigh. "Window dressing for the board."

"I think we're far enough away that we can't be heard."

She didn't respond. He was right. Voices were too distant to make out any conversation and the band was playing, so anything they said would be drowned out by the music. She listened to the tune the band was playing. It was something she recognized. "Blue Moon," an old favorite of her grandfather's. Though the melody was still very recognizable, it was being played with a more animated rhythm. She decided she liked it.

Unconsciously, she scanned the indigo sky. The moon above them was neither blue nor full—but a wide crescent of gold, hanging suspended above the highest swaying boughs of the red mangrove and feathery palms. The breeze was salty yet overlaid with the floral scents of an equatorial night. She inhaled deeply, knowing she was living out as romantic a scene as any woman could hope for.

She cast a surreptitious gaze at the man beside her. His profile was rugged yet somber. The ocean breeze had tossed a swath of silvery hair across his forehead, making him seem almost accessible. She felt an unwelcome upwelling of attraction for him, and had an urge to reach up and smooth his hair into place. Hurriedly, she turned away, fighting the impulse.

They'd moved into comparative darkness. Waves swirled around Mercy's ankles as they shambled through the eddying tide. Damon was on the ocean side, and she was glad, for she didn't swim well, and didn't relish the idea of being swept out to sea on an undertow.

A piercing pain in her foot made her cry out.

"What is it?" he asked.

"I don't know." Unthinking, she put her weight on him, lifting her foot to inspect it. Before she could see what was wrong, he'd lifted her in his arms and was carrying her toward dry sand.

He strode with her to the edge of the forest where he ripped a couple of palmetto leaves from a palm. Placing them on the sand, he lowered her to one while he sat down on the other. "Here, let me see." He took her injured foot in his hands.

She tried to withdraw, feeling foolish.

"Don't," he cautioned. "If it's a sea urchin spine, you'll need treatment."

She chewed the inside of her cheek as he examined her foot. "It—it's better already," she insisted. "I don't think it was anything, really."

His hands were so warm against her wet flesh, she almost forgot the pain as he probed and stroked, removing sand to have a better look. "I think you may have just stepped on a broken shell. How does it feel now? Any stinging?"

She swallowed, wanting to say, *It's never felt better,* but she knew that wouldn't be very bright. "Fine," she croaked, embarrassed that she'd acted like such a sissy. "I—I think you're right about it being a broken shell. I was just jumpy. I don't know what sort of things lurk in the ocean."

He smiled then, his white teeth amazingly clear in the

darkness. "Little Miss Midwest meets the big, bad ocean."

A blush fired her cheeks, and she was thankful he couldn't see it in the darkness. "Something like that, I guess." She watched as he drew up a knee and encircled an arm around it, getting comfortable. Suddenly nervous, she shot a glance over her shoulder toward the lighted area where the party was going on. A tall, irregular outcropping of rock blocked her view. She whirled to face him, demanding, "Is this another ploy of yours? Are they supposed to think we're making love?"

His smile faded and he glanced back toward the party. It seemed clear from his expression that he hadn't planned any such thing. He'd merely set her down to examine her foot. His chuckle brought her back and she focused on him. "That's what it'll look like, all right," he admitted. "Do you mind?"

Her poise was little more than a thin shell about her now. Being out here alone with Damon under a tropical moon was difficult enough on her nerves. But the idea of having thirty people think she was having wild sex with him on the beach made her absolutely crazy!

On the other hand, she was *supposed* to be married, *supposed* to be on her honeymoon. Making love on a moonlit beach with the man you loved was one of the most romantic notions in the world. If they were truly newlyweds, they would very likely be doing just that.

Trying for a nonchalant shrug, she muttered, "I guess I don't mind. It's no worse a lie than anything else we've let them believe." She had a sudden idea, and was rankled enough by this whole bizarre situation to ask. "Have you made love to many other women on moonlit beaches?''

His eyes narrowed speculatively. "*Other* women?"

That word "other," and the taunting way he'd uttered it, hit her in the pit of her stomach like a hot rock. She squirmed at the sizzling feeling it elicited. Why had she asked the question that way? It made her inquiry sound as though she expected him to make love to *her*, too! "I—I meant..." Infuriated by his ability to fluster her so with one mild query, she snapped, "You know what I meant!"

The beginnings of a grin touched his mouth. "I don't know, Ms. Stewart."

"Of course you do!" she insisted. "It's as plain as—"

"I mean, I don't know how many women I've made love to on moonlit beaches."

That admission stopped her. Dropping her gaze, she began to toy with the tie of her skirt. "Oh..." she breathed, so humiliated she couldn't face him. He'd made love to so many women that even in the subcategory of "moonlit beaches" he couldn't remember them all! She had an overpowering urge to scream, but she squelched it.

Well aware that she was acting like a silly schoolgirl, she forced herself to stop messing with her tie and sit up straight, though she couldn't quite face him. Trying for nonchalance, she challenged, "I—I suppose a playboy like you would be very proud of—"

"Quiet," he ordered under his breath.

She snapped her head around to look at him and opened her mouth to ask him what his problem was, but he halted her by holding two fingers before his mouth.

He'd twisted to stare toward the party and seemed intent on something.

She turned, too, but saw nothing out of the ordinary. "What is it?" she finally asked, her curiosity getting the best of her.

Frowning, he waited a few more seconds, then commanded, "Wait here." He got up and soundlessly loped to the colossal boulder that protruded from the forest. When he got there, he edged around it to check the other side. Mercy's stomach constricted when she understood what he was doing. *He thought someone had been eavesdropping!* After another half minute, he reappeared and came back to settle beside her.

"Find anything?" she asked.

He shook his head.

"You didn't see anybody? Any tracks?"

"Hell." He shrugged. "There are tracks all over. People have been all over this beach all day."

"Do you think anybody could have heard us from there?"

He nodded. "I think so."

"Oh, no," she moaned.

"It's possible it was just a turtle crawling into the brush."

She pulled her knees up and hugged them. "I hope so."

"If it wasn't, we'll know soon enough."

She rested her chin on her knees and closed her eyes. "Maybe we didn't say anything incriminating," she offered hopefully.

He chucked morosely. "We're not making love, Ms. Stewart. That's incriminating enough."

She twisted to glare at him, horrified. But quickly enough, she realized he was right. It was ironic that she had to worry that someone might have caught her *not* having sex. What an impossible position their lie had put them in!

Out of the night came the tawny-throated warble of a familiar birdcall. "Mockingbird," she mumbled, forcing her thoughts to less distressing things.

"They're called nightingales here," Damon said.

"Really?" She listened, finding her spirits lift at the sound. "It's a pretty word—nightingale."

" 'The little live nightingale had come to sing of comfort and hope,' " he began quietly, contemplatively, and Mercy realized he was quoting from something. He went on. " 'As he sang, the phantoms grew pale, and still more pale, and the blood flowed quicker and quicker through the Emperor's feeble body. Even Death listened and said, "Go on, little nightingale, go on"!' "

Mercy faced him. His expression was sober. "What was that from? It's lovely."

"Hans Christian Andersen," he said. "I probably misquoted. It's been a long time since mother used to—" He stopped himself, gritted his teeth and looked away.

Mercy knew his family was a sore subject with him, but she had to ask, "Your mother read to you when you were a boy?"

He didn't answer, merely stared out at the undulating sea. For a long time all she could hear was the distant reggae interpretation of "Strangers in the Night," the slow swishing water washing along the sand, and the faint sigh of the trade winds in the treetops.

"Damon," she tried again. "I'm sorry you lost your parents—"

"I didn't *lose* my parents," he cut in, grinding out the words contemptuously. Then he laughed, a bitter, empty sound. "Oh, they died in a boating accident, all right. But they'd shipped me off years before...." He faced her again, his features hard. "*Damn it.* I hate this place."

Abruptly he stood, and instinctively she did, too, her heart going out to him. She couldn't begin to understand what had happened to make his parents desert him, and clearly he couldn't understand it, either. She watched in the darkness as his jaw worked in frustration and long-buried grief.

With his childhood wound so visible, she forgot she disliked him, forgot that his family had caused her grandfather a lifetime of heartache, and took his large hand in both of hers. "I'm sorry, Damon," she offered helplessly. Not knowing what to do, she simply tugged on his fingers. "Sit down. Let's enjoy the night and try to forget—everything else." She tugged again, returning to her seat on the palm leaf.

He glanced at her, his features grim. She was still holding his hand with both of hers, refusing to let go. Urging again with another gentle pull, she decided to try to lighten the situation, and teased, "We wouldn't want to go back too quickly. Assuming it really was a turtle you heard, we're *still* supposed to be newlyweds. What kind of a bridegroom takes five minutes?"

He grunted out a humorless chuckle. "It's kind of you to consider my ego, Ms. Stewart." Sitting back down, he stared out to sea.

She hesitantly let go of his fingers and leaned back on her hands, digging her nails into the sand in an attempt to scrape away the touch of his skin against hers. "You forget, Mr. DeMorney, my ego's at stake, too. What sort of a bride would I be if I couldn't keep your attention for longer than five minutes?"

He drew up a leg and circled his knee with his arms. This time his chuckle was deeper, more genuine. When he glanced her way, his lips quirked pleasantly, sending a strange thrill along her spine. "How long do you think our egos need to stay out here?" he asked.

His wry question let her see the absurdity of the whole situation and brought a grin to her face, too. "Thirty minutes?"

He leaned back, stretching out his long, muscular legs. "The male ego is a delicate mechanism, Ms. Stewart. I'd say, at least an hour."

She laughed. "Too bad we didn't bring a deck of cards."

"Too bad you're a virgin or we could really make love."

She'd glanced toward the darkened ocean, but when he said that, she turned to gape at him. He was watching her, his grin teasing. "Or do you want to insist again that you're not."

She pulled up onto her knees and belligerently faced him. "Do you seriously suggest that you know women who'd make love to you on the beach, simply to pass an hour?"

His grin grew wider. "You continue to amaze me," he taunted softly. "Of course I know women like that."

"*Well,*" she scoffed, "if you want my opinion, you've been hanging around with the wrong kind of women!"

He laughed openly, a mellow sound that affected her against her will. *Of course he knew that kind of woman,* her mind berated. He was so gorgeous, so charismatic, she had no doubt that he could even turn other kinds of women into *that* kind of woman. He was sitting very close to one woman who was *not* that kind, but might throw herself into his lap at any second and become that kind if she weren't severely stern with herself right *now!*

"We could look for constellations, if you'd rather," he offered, laughter in his voice.

"What!" she flung back, only to realize her tone was a bit harsh for his harmless suggestion.

He was shrugging off his shirt, which worried her until he laid it on the sand behind her and gestured. "Use this so your back won't get sandy." Even as he said it, he lay down beside her, cupping his head with a hand. With the other, he pointed toward the sky. "That's Canis Major."

She eyed him dubiously for a moment, but decided he was serious about looking at stars. She lay down on his shirt and squinted in the direction he was pointing. "Where?"

"Near Puppis."

"Oh, near *Puppis,*" she quipped, making it clear from her tone she had no idea where Puppis might be.

He shifted her way. "Canis Major contains the star Sirius, if that helps."

"Immensely," she returned, having no idea what he was talking about.

"What about the Big Dipper? Can you find that one?"

She examined the sky, quickly spotting it. She was relieved, because half the time she couldn't even locate that one—the easiest constellation to find. She pointed. "There it is."

"Good girl. Little Dipper?"

"No idea."

He chuckled. "You're going to have to try harder, Ms. Stewart. At this rate, we're not going to need an hour."

She glanced at him and was disconcerted to see that his eyes were on her rather than the heavens. "I guess I'm— I'm not much good at stargazing," she murmured, her voice going fragile and shaky.

"I'll help." He lifted up on one elbow. "The Little Dipper contains the seven brightest stars in the constellation Ursa Minor. Look, there."

She turned in the direction he pointed, but didn't see any particular seven stars that looked all that bright. "How do you know so much about stars?" she asked.

"I don't. You just know less than I do."

She peered at him. The charming grin he flashed seemed so real—nothing forced or phony for onlookers—and she responded to it, shivering with feminine appreciation.

"Are you cold?" he asked, sounding closer.

She pulled her lip between her teeth, wondering why part of the sky was suddenly blocked from her vision. After a few erratic heartbeats, it occurred to her strangely numbed brain that he was nearer, looming above her. She shook her head. "I—I'm not cold. . . ." On the contrary, she was growing deliciously warm from the radiant heat of his body.

"Mercy..." The murmur of her given name out here in private, away from everyone, seemed as intimate as a caress.

"Hmm?" She couldn't get her lips to move, so the questioning sound was the best she could do.

"I'm going to kiss you."

She swallowed. She'd sensed his intention before he'd said a word, and she had no idea why she was allowing this. Crazed, weak-minded female that she was, she *wanted* him to kiss her, couldn't find a shred of resistance to the idea. That was illogical, counter to everything she'd ever thought or said or hoped! Yet none of that mattered at this moment, not with his powerful body so near, his eyes so beguiling.

His statement of intent hung in the air between them, unanswered for what seemed like hours. Evidently he was giving her a chance to cut and run, to act like the fainthearted virgin he thought her to be. If she could have formed a coherent response, she would have told him she had no intention of going anywhere. But as it was, she couldn't move or speak. She could only stare up at him, mute invitation in her eyes.

CHAPTER SEVEN

WHEN HE TILTED HIS HEAD toward her, she amazed herself by reaching up to meet his lips halfway. His kiss was warm, but not as demanding as he'd been in public. Sliding her arms about his neck, she coaxed him to blanket her with his body. He followed her down, kissing her softly, sensitively, yet she could feel his powerful body shudder with pent-up tension as though he was holding back, not wanting to frighten her, overwhelm her because of her innocence.

The tender beauty of the experience made her want to be closer to him, to taste him more deeply. Instinctively she opened her mouth, inviting greater intimacy.

He stilled, lifting his lips to hover just above hers. "Mercy," he groaned, "don't tempt me."

She was having none of his chivalrous self-restraint now. His kiss had been wildly stimulating even as fleeting and disciplined as it had been. She craved knowing a wilder, more intense excitement she sensed he was capable of evoking—*if he wanted to.*

"Kiss me, Damon," she urged through a sigh. *"Really kiss me."* Fearing he might further object, she met his lips with wanton abandon. It wasn't as though she'd never been kissed, for heaven's sake. He needn't treat her like a china doll. Parting her lips willfully, she dared him to possess her mouth.

The sound that issued up from his throat was half chuckle, half groan. Parting his lips in a like manner, he teased and tempted, his movements lazy and shockingly sensuous. She felt a fierce, aching thrill at the seductiveness of his kiss as it deepened, his questing tongue sending her spiraling toward new stirrings, heightened needs.

She clung to him, wanting the intimacy to go on and on. The naked strength of his rippling back beneath her fingers made her tremble with anticipation. He was so large, so exciting, and he was going to make love to her, too—here on the beach. She knew deep in her heart that she would never, ever forget his mastery over—

Her mind tumbled and slipped, trying to focus on something very important. What was it? Damon was going to make love to her here on the beach—too...

Too!

That was the word that held the truth she didn't want to face. Visions of countless women writhing on the beach in Damon's arms flashed in her mind. *Legions of women.* So many women Damon couldn't even guess at a number. And she was about to join that long list! Where had her good sense gone? He'd tried to leave it with one experimental kiss, but *no,* she'd insisted. And now his bare chest was crushing her breasts, the heat of his body searing her flesh. His knowledge of how to pleasure a woman was astonishing, so much so that even that first, brief kiss had drugged her mind, sent her teetering on the edge of sanity.

Damon was no longer holding back, assuming she'd given her consent. A voice nagged that she'd done just that, but she shoved the realization aside. *"No..."* she cried, but it came out sounding like a passion-drenched sigh. And her arms were still clutching, clinging to his back, acting on a need and will of their own. What kind of a dimwit was she? "Oh, Damon," she tried again when he lifted his lips from hers to move in a lush, nipping exploration along her jaw and throat.

His teeth and lips left her tingling with sweet urgency, and she could only open her lips in mute protest as he paid stimulating homage to the pulsing hollow of her throat.

His lips left a moist, sizzling trail as he traveled farther down to feast on the rise of one breast. The shock of imminent surrender gave her her voice, and she cried, "Damon—*don't....*" It had taken all her ebbing strength to force those two words from between her benumbed, throbbing lips. She wasn't sure he'd even heard her, the plea had been so frail and breathy.

After another second it was clear that he had, for his kisses stopped and he lifted his mouth slightly away from her skin, though his breath still tantalized her flesh. She'd regained enough control to open her eyes and look at him. Focusing on the silvery beauty of his hair, she had an urge to run her fingers through it. She knew it would feel heavenly between her fingers, but she resisted. With great effort, she dragged her arms away from his back. "Damon," she repeated, her voice still far from normal. "Please..."

His low, irascible chuckle surprised her as he lifted himself up to linger above her, his gaze narrow. "Don't ever tell me you're not a virgin, again, Ms. Stewart," he admonished gruffly. With that, he rolled away and sat up.

She could only lie there, staring at him with baffled wariness. He'd let her go so easily. What had she expected, a fight? Objections?

He wasn't looking at her now, but was staring out to sea, a hard expression on his face. She sensed a supercharged tension in the air between them, and was suddenly struck by the truth. It wasn't that Damon found her undesirable. He simply didn't force a woman to have sex with him once she'd said *no*. Looking closer at his profile, she could tell by the clenching and unclenching of his jaw that he'd been as affected by the near seduction as she, and was working at regaining control.

It was an ironic time to do so, but she found that insight into his character terribly attractive and was almost sorry she'd put a stop to—everything. He was a surprisingly sensitive man beneath all his bold arrogance, and she sensed he would be a caring lover. Struggling to sit up, she was stunned at how wobbly she felt. "Thank you, Damon," she offered.

He flicked her a cynical glance. "For what?"

"You know." She shrugged, wishing she had the nerve to touch his hand in gratitude, but knowing it would be the absolute wrong thing to do. "For being so gallant. I've known men who weren't half so nice about it."

He mouthed a curse, running a distracted hand through his moonlit hair. "I kissed you. It was my fault." Pushing himself up to stand, he held out a hand. "We'd better get back. I think my ego's had enough of a workout tonight."

She would have avoided his touch, but knew she was too shaky to stand on her own. He affected her so thoroughly; his kisses were debilitating—deliciously so. When she placed her fingers in his, he helped her to stand. Dipping down, he picked up his shirt and placed it about her shoulders. She was grateful, for it was getting chilly. "Thanks," she murmured without looking at him.

They walked side by side for a few minutes before he placed his hand about her waist again. "Don't panic," he cautioned, derision in his tone.

"Why are you angry?" she asked, peering sideways at him. "Or is that what sexual frustration does to a man?"

He frowned down at her. "I've never heard of sexual frustration as a remedy for headaches. Does that answer your question?"

A giggle bubbled up in her throat and she was startled by it. "Sorry," she whispered. No doubt her tattered nerves were getting the better of her.

He grunted. "You have an interesting sense of humor."

"I'm not laughing at you," she insisted. "I think—I could be having a nervous breakdown from all the stress. I don't even like you, and I almost—we almost..."

His frown deepened. "You're not having a nervous breakdown. You're experiencing what *almost* having sex does to virgins."

She sobered. "You're such an expert on virgins?"

"Let's change the damn subject."

Unable to let it drop, she demanded, "How many virgins have you deflowered?"

"Forty-two at last count."

She stumbled to a halt. "That's disgusting!"

"Hell!" He turned on her. "It's also crap. If I were the womanizer everyone thought I was, I wouldn't have time to eat, let alone run a business."

She stared at him, his unexpected admission defusing her ire. "You wouldn't?"

He shook his head at her obvious stupefaction. "Come on."

"Well, how many, then—really?"

He exhaled loudly. "Even if you were my wife, it wouldn't be your business."

She flushed. "Did you promise any of *them* marriage?"

"I promised them whatever they wanted to hear."

She whirled to stare at him.

He half grinned at her horrified expression. "Promises are made to be broken, Ms. Stewart," he remarked with a contemptuous flare of his nostrils. "I learned that lesson early and well."

"And—and what of their feelings when you broke those promises?"

"What of them?" he asked without inflection, turning away.

She felt his arm encircle her waist again, and shuddered, but not from dislike of the man, from the pain she'd seen flash across his face, the sadness shading his words. *Good heavens, what had done this to him?* What had wounded him so badly that it made him so contemptuous of intimate relationships?

Without hesitation, she wrapped her arm about his waist, really wanting to for the first time. She wished she had whatever power he needed to heal the tragic gash in his soul. "Damon?" she asked after a few strained minutes. "Why didn't you make me some empty promises back there—to have your way with me on the beach? Surely you could tell I was—weakening."

She could feel his muscles tense at her question, but his step didn't falter. By now they were nearing the party-goers, and the band was playing a lively version of "Bad Boys," a popular reggae tune.

"Damon," she coaxed. "Why? And don't say it was because you didn't want me, because I could tell you did."

He stopped and turned to fully face her. His lips lifted in a cynical smile, but the expression held a suggestion of melancholy. He scanned her face for a long minute. Finally he reached up to graze her hair with his fingers. Surprising her, he took her into his arms to dance. "You have sand in your hair, darling," he murmured, his breath teasing her temple.

As he held her against his chest, she could feel the strong beat of his heart, and she relished their closeness, even against her will. From the corner of her eye, she noticed that several of his stockholders had drawn near enough so that Damon was no longer at liberty to speak freely.

Or did he simply have no answer for her question?

DAMON SAT in his yacht's luxurious office, fitted with every possible electronic device a business tycoon might need, including satellite communications, computers, fax machines, color printers and copiers. It was late, and he was tired, but he wanted to go over the daily sales figures, even though his mind wasn't on them. His thoughts drifted as he stared at his hand and the four Caymanian coins Otis had given him earlier that evening. They weren't worth more than one American dollar, but the old man had gone to so much trouble to deliver them.

He fingered the silver pieces, turning them in his fingers, wondering about the man who'd so painstakingly limped to the water's edge all the way from the house, to present them—along with a feeble hug.

His stare drilled into those damned coins and he fisted his hand around them, angry at the memories they conjured. His own grandfather had never hugged him. The cold bastard. Damon had been nothing to him but a means to an end. When Kennard's son had proved ill equipped for the job, Damon had become Kennard's last hope—the young prince who would succeed him as king of his automotive empire. Damon had been raised precisely for that purpose, like a champion stallion bred for speed and strength. Never once could he recall being hugged by his grandfather—just drilled, rebuked, molded, then forged in the kiln of Kennard's iron will.

Opening his fingers, he scowled at the coins, irritated that his mind kept slipping to them and to Mercy's grandfather. He was so devoted to her, and it was laughable how devoted Mercy was to him—trying to pull off her preposterous scheme to clear his name. Unfortunately for her, she couldn't lie her way out of a paper bag.

He was arrested from his dark musings when searching hands reached from behind him to slip down his shoulders and seductively skim his chest. He lifted his head with a jerk, startled by Mercy's sudden show of passion. When she'd left him an hour ago, she'd seemed somehow warmer toward him, not quite so antagonistic. He was still confused about the softening in her attitude, yet he'd had no idea such sexy plans had been going through her brain. Maybe she was harder to read than he'd thought.

"Well, hello," he murmured. With a swell of masculine gratification, he took her wrist, pulling her around his leather swivel chair. It jolted him when the woman he'd coaxed into his lap wasn't his unpredictable make-believe bride, but his extremely predictable cousin by marriage, Buffy Leyland.

"Hello, yourself, stranger." She snaked her arms about his neck. "I'm glad to see the excitement of having a new bride has worn off. Now maybe you'll have time for me." Her mouth was very near bloodred and open in an inviting pout.

He offered her a twisted grin. "I gather your mourning period for Mitchell is over?"

She laughed, the purr of a cat anticipating cream. "Don't pretend to be disapproving," she cajoled. "You and Mitchell were never close. He simply hated you, you know."

Damon lifted a brow. "Really?"

She toyed with the hair at his nape. "I don't blame him. You beat him at everything in school—president of the senior class, captain of the football team, you got all the cheerleaders. . . ." She leaned closer to kiss the edge of his mouth. "It always made me wonder if you were better than Mitchell at—everything. . . ."

Damon sat still as she brushed the other corner of his mouth with hers. "Hmm?" she urged, coyly pressing her bikini-clad breasts against his bare chest. "He would have voted against you in favor of Clayton if he'd lived."

"And what about you?" he queried, knowing full well what she was going to suggest.

She shifted away to judge his expression, which he was careful to keep amicable. Smiling, apparently satisfied so far, she said, "Oh—I'm still trying to make up my mind. I thought—if we met privately—you might convince me to swing my votes your way." She paused, her smile going sly. "I'd hate to go against Mitchell's wishes without good reason."

"I can see that," he said, hard-pressed to keep the disgust from his voice.

He could feel her stiffen then, and though she held on to her smile, he saw a flicker of worry in her eyes. She wasn't convinced he was buying it. But it was clear she had no intention of giving up. "How would you feel about a walk on the beach?" she cooed, stroking his earlobe. "I'm a very good—listener."

He surveyed her face. She was a beauty, with fashion-model cheekbones, a pert, turned-up nose, and full lips—painted red and slightly opened the way they were—well, the erotic symbolism was hardly lost on him. Buffy had the sort of voluptuous body every healthy man dreamed of burying himself inside. He'd heard rumors for years of how freely she gave away her hedonistic favors, and tonight she was practically begging to give Damon an exhilarating ride—and in the bargain, her corporate votes. Not a bad night's work.

Instead of feeling pleased with the offer, he was very sorry for Mitchell. Though there had never been any love lost between the two cousins, Damon found himself pitying the man, wondering how he'd stood living with this self-centered cheat.

Granting her his most charming smile, he assisted her off his lap, then stood. "I think a walk would be nice." Taking her hand, he led her from the office, then down the hallway to the foyer and onto the deck. The breeze was cool, salty, and seemed sweet and pure compared to the cloying perfume Buffy wore. He helped her down the gangway, then drew her hand to his lips.

"What's this?" she asked through a giggle.

"It's good night," he said, releasing her. "Have a nice walk."

"But, Damon—"

"Buffy," he interrupted, this time allowing his irritation to register in his tone. "Mitchell hated me. Feel free to do the same."

"But—but, Damon," she cried. "You need my votes!"

"Yes, I do," he returned.

"Then why?"

He glanced down at his hand, the one that clutched the damnable coins. "Hell if I know." Lifting his gaze to her thunderstruck features, he indicated with a nod that she leave. "If you'll excuse me, I have a call to make." Turning his back, he bounded up the gangway and headed toward his office.

DAMON HAD GONE directly from the party to his office, nearly an hour ago. Mercy had known there was no way she could sleep. Her nerves were too overwrought. So she'd showered and put on the most conventional of the lingerie Aunt Jo had forced her to purchase, a white silk gown that reached all the way to her ankles. It was daringly sheer, following the contours of her body to a disturbingly accurate degree. Even with the matching silk wrap, the ensemble was indecent.

She tried to read a novel, but her mind kept moving on its own to thoughts of Damon—his kiss, his anger, his quiet pain. She finally tossed the book down in aggravation and slid from the bed, deciding to go out on the aft deck to try to calm her nerves with the rare beauty of a tropical night.

She'd almost reached the double doors that led to the deck when a noise distracted her from her course. She turned in time to see Damon leading Buffy along the hallway—*her hand in his*—toward the foyer.

She stilled in the shadows as they stealthily moved toward the exit. Ice spread through her veins. So *this* was what he'd been doing in his office late into the night! She bit her lip. *Mercy, what are you getting so up in arms about? The man's not your husband. He has every right to seek out female companionship if he cares to. Don't be a jealous fool.*

She found herself moving toward the foyer. Exactly why, she had no idea. When she reached the door that led to the deck, she cracked it open. Damon and Buffy were on the dock now, and Damon was kissing her hand.

With Buffy's giggle echoing in her ears, Mercy soundlessly closed the door and slumped against the bulwark. Unable to fathom the dull ache that had begun pounding in her temples, she made her way to the master suite and closed the door at her back.

A half hour passed—or a hundred years—Mercy couldn't be sure as she lay in the darkened cabin, staring out the picture window at a placid, moon-spangled ocean. Unfortunately the tranquil scene did nothing for her infuriated state, and that infuriated her even more. She had no right to be upset about Damon's choice of sexual partners. He was doing her a favor by going along with her lie. He owed her nothing! Of course he wasn't doing any harm to his chances of keeping his company under his leadership, either. And probably, tonight, he'd enhanced those chances further, as far as Buffy's votes were concerned.

She gritted her teeth against the vision of the two of them together, and tried to think of other things—of Otis's doctor saying that her grandpa would be fine with Aunt Jo's tender loving care—of her grandfather and Aunt Jo living happily for years and years, trailed by frolicking pigs. Darn that doctor. Why did he have to choose this week to be out of town!

Mercy heard the unmistakable click of the door opening. Damon was coming to bed. She snapped her eyes shut, feigning sleep.

She could hear him cross the room and enter his bath. When his head door closed, she opened her eyes again and glared at the closed portal. Once the shower came on, she forced herself to turn away, trying to will herself to sleep. She didn't care to be awake when he came out. She might have an overwhelming urge to leap up and congratulate him on successfully winning Buffy's votes—*and everything else she had to offer.*

When he came out fifteen minutes later, she was still awake, and very sorry about it, especially when he walked around to stand before the window wall. Sensing where he'd gone by the faint brush of his footsteps, she covertly opened her eyes. His back to her, he was staring out to sea. A massive, compelling silhouette against the misty moon glow, his thick, silvery hair gleamed and his shoulders blotted out a great deal of the starry sky. He wore only a pair of dark nylon shorts, and his long, sturdy legs were braced wide. She had the fanciful thought that no Viking warrior or Indian brave had ever looked so potent or desirable in the moonlight.

Though she knew he was unscrupulous in his use of women, she couldn't help but admit he was a delicious sight. Unable to help herself, she stared at her tall, handsome antagonist towering there—all power and muscle—wishing she could simply close her eyes and forget that he existed.

Suddenly he bowed his head and mumbled a raw curse. She was puzzled, wondering what dark thoughts were going through his mind. He looked down at his wristwatch, evidently checking the time. He turned then, and she squeezed her eyes tight, trying to persuade her breathing to be slow, even, faking normalcy. Her task was made harder when she noticed he was moving *toward* her.

Sensing his nearness, she fretted about what he might be doing. She made herself continue to breathe—in, out, in, out—working to keep her breaths deliberate and uniform, praying he wouldn't detect that she was not only awake, but that every nerve in her body was tingling with a blend of anticipation and dread. Why was he standing above her? He had to be studying her. But *why?*

A shrill ringing broke the night silence, and Mercy was amazed that she managed to keep from leaping up and screaming. If she jumped at all, Damon must have missed it when he'd turned his attention to the noise.

He rounded the bed and jerked up the receiver on the phone. "Yes?" he whispered. After a brief pause he said, "Shamus, I'm glad your answering service found you. I need something done, but I can't talk here. Give me a second to get to another phone."

There was a faint clatter as he set down the receiver. A couple of seconds later, he was gone.

Mercy opened her eyes and turned to look at the phone—the receiver was off the hook, lying on the table. In the stillness, she imagined she could almost distinguish voices. Twisting away, she squeezed her eyes shut. The call was none of her business. Still, she couldn't ignore it. She'd recognized the name Shamus. He was the head of Panther Automotive's legal staff. Aunt Jo had spoken of him—"Famous Amos Shamus," she'd called him, referring to him as one of the most brilliant corporate lawyers in the country.

Rolling over, she stared at the receiver, dim in the darkness, her heart hammering in her ears. If there was even the slightest possibility Damon was speaking to his lawyer about—she could hardly bring herself to even think of the idea—*about an audit of the books back when Otis was fired?*

This was something her mother had dreamed of most of her life, something Mercy had hoped for with all her being. Beside herself with longing that it be true, she gave up her attempts to disregard the call and scrambled across the bed. Very stealthily, she bent to place her ear as close to the receiver as she could. Her heart in her throat, she stopped breathing, listening.

"But a forty-year-old audit, Damon?" a gravelly voice was shouting. "That will be nearly impossible—"

"Damn it, Amos," Damon interrupted. "When I want *easy,* I'll hire a first-year law student. Just handle it." There was a loud click in Mercy's ear as Damon severed the connection.

She straightened, her mind clouded with amazement. He was really going to do it! Damon was *really* going to get to the bottom of Otis's firing! She clutched her hands to her breasts, her heart filling with such gratitude—such affection—she wanted to rush into his arms, kiss him soundly. She'd been so wrong about him. Just because he was rich, tough-minded and successful, didn't mean he couldn't also be a fair, honest man.

She heard a creaking sound and realized Damon must be coming back. Jumping into the bed, she clambered to the far side and slid beneath the covers. A heartbeat later, he entered the room. After another second she heard the phone's receiver being replaced in its cradle. A few seconds later he climbed into his makeshift bunk.

Mercy covertly shifted her gaze to where he was lying and smiled tremulously at his reclining form. A grateful tear trickled along her cheek. New feelings of softness blossomed in her breast for the man—soft feelings mixed with remorse.

She hadn't allowed herself to face it until this minute, but it suddenly hit her hard in the pit of her stomach. With what she'd learned about Damon DeMorney in the past week, she'd grown fond of him against her will. And now, with this unexpected noble deed, she feared she might be on the brink of falling . . .

She squeezed her eyes shut, choking back a moan, unable to even complete the idea in her mind. Such an improbable match was laughable, even to her.

CHAPTER EIGHT

WITH A NEW BUOYANCY in her heart, Mercy was up before first light the next morning. Her gratitude was so great she'd hardly slept all night. So she resolved that activity was the best answer to her restlessness. She wanted to physically do something for Damon, and she knew the thing she wanted to do most—*physically*—would be damaging for her emotions in the long run, so she compromised, deciding the very least she could do was make him a good breakfast.

By the time the sun was shooting vertical beams from behind clouds clustered on the horizon, Mercy returned to their suite, her wicker tray loaded down with a hearty breakfast of waffles and maple syrup, sautéed tomatoes, poached finnan haddie, and a steaming carafe of coffee.

As she knelt beside the settee to rouse Damon, the beginning sprawl of orange fire burst from the edge of the sea, basking the room in a peachy glow.

Mercy stilled as the morning light paid quiet respect to Damon's masculine good looks. His skin glowed bronze; his hair shimmered a magical color—like ice on fire. Silver-tipped lashes languished across the hollows below his eyes, hollows that appeared slightly bluish even in the blush of dawn. Mercy was distressed to see the exhaustion that showed in his face during his unguarded moments. Yet, even as weary as his rough-cut features were, there was a stark beauty there, and she couldn't help but devour him with her eyes.

Her glance drifted to his lips, firm and slightly open, almost in invitation. Again she saw the tiny, white scar on his mouth. Flushing, she remembered the first time she'd seen that scar and had kissed him in her overmedicated state, thinking to make it well. Abashed at the recollection, she pulled her lips between her teeth, growing hot with a yearning to know the touch of those lips again, to kiss him in gratitude for what he was doing for her grandfather.

She didn't dare think about her decision, fearing she'd change her mind if logic intruded. Hurriedly, she lowered her tray to the floor and bent to brush his lips with her own. The contact filled her with a giddy hunger to know his tender caresses, his unrestrained lovemaking, and that knowledge knocked her back on her heels. It wasn't a very bright thing to want, but there she sat, throbbing with desire for one of the world's *most* desirable men. She slumped there, her hands icy on her burning cheeks, as she attempted to calm her breathing.

She heard him stir, and her gaze rocketed to his face. His eyelids were twitching and he shifted his head toward the light. She held her breath, unable to do anything but watch as he woke up. He blinked a couple of times, then seemed to register that someone was hovering nearby. When he squinted to focus on her, she flinched inwardly.

Trying to smile as though it was the most ordinary thing in the world for her to be crouched beside him while he slept, she mumbled, "Oh—you're awake."

Looking charmingly groggy, he ran a hand through his dawn-burnished hair. "If you don't want to wake a man, Ms. Stewart, don't kiss him."

The fact that he knew what she'd done appalled her and she was glad the crimson flush of sunrise hid her humiliation. "I—I didn't kiss you!" It was a flimsy lie, but her other choices were worse. She couldn't bear for him to know she was so stupidly attracted to him that she dared kiss him while he slept. Or the other reason—her gratitude. She couldn't risk admitting her eavesdropping. He already thought of her as underhanded enough. Besides, she wanted Damon to tell her his good deed in his own way.

Tawny brows lifted mockingly. "I suppose it is safer for virgins to kiss unconscious men, but I can't imagine that it's very satisfying."

With renewed embarrassment, she looked away. Even unconscious, his kiss had stimulated her more than she cared to admit. However, she had no intention of divulging that information. She'd experienced enough humiliation for one sunrise. Instead she bent to retrieve the breakfast tray. "Here," she snapped, unceremoniously plopping it in the general area of his lap, since much of his body was hidden by a sheet. "I made you breakfast." Pushing up, she gave him a huffy glance and marched toward the exit.

"Why did you—"

"I told you!" she flung back, spinning to face him. "I did *not* kiss you!"

He sat up and the sheet slipped down to expose his chest. "I meant, why did you make me breakfast?" he corrected softly, amusement in his tone. He swung his legs to the floor and adjusted the tray, never moving his eyes from her face.

Somehow that disconcerted her almost as much as the fact that she had been more preoccupied with the kiss than he. "Why? Because—because I..." Again she toyed with the idea of telling him she'd eavesdropped on his phone conversation and knew the wonderful thing he was doing for Otis. For a second time, she decided against it. Surely he would want to tell her what he'd done himself. Clasping her hands before her, she stuttered, "I—I guess I fixed your breakfast because I've concluded you're not the corrupt monster I thought you were—after all."

The humor in his gaze flickered out. "I'm flattered," he muttered, his tone sarcastic.

Having difficulty holding eye contact, she hurried on. "And—uh—I wish you luck with your stock vote thing. You were right, before. I *don't* like Clayton Stringman." She wanted to add that she didn't like his friend, Buffy, either, but knew her opinion on that subject would be far from appropriate. After all, she and Damon weren't *really* married. He had a right to find feminine companionship wherever he wanted.

His expression grew perplexed. "Ms. Stewart, did something happen last night that I missed?"

She managed a faint smile at the irony of his question. Something very definite happened last night. Something merciful and unselfish and remarkable, and he knew exactly what it was. Unable to stand it anymore, she decided to urge the issue along. "Is—is there anything you want to tell me?"

He inclined his head as though considering the pros and cons of divulging something. "Well," he began, and

Mercy's heart skipped a beat. *Here it comes!* "I wasn't going to mention this, but you have a little flour on your nose."

Her excitement evaporated. The wide smile she'd presented quickly died, and she could only stare, deflated and tongue-tied.

"Oh, and thanks for the breakfast—Messy Miss," he added with a wry grin.

Ignoring the taunt, she stared at him, confused about why he was keeping the audit a secret. Then in a flash it occurred to her. *Of course!* He didn't want her to worry—in case he found evidence against Otis. That was ridiculous, naturally. Her grandfather would be found completely innocent. Still it was sweet of Damon to be concerned. She took a deep breath, feeling better, and rediscovered her smile. "I understand," she murmured. "No problem. I'll go clean the galley."

This time it was his turn to lose his grin. "You understand what?" he queried.

She was oblivious to what he'd asked, her mind working a mile a minute. If he was going to be so considerate, then the least she could do was to be considerate of him. "Is there anything we're doing tonight that I should know about?" she asked, determined to be fully prepared for anything.

"Just dinner around the pool." He was eyeing her curiously.

She nodded, self-consciously rubbing the back of her hand across her smudged nose. Even though their newlywed devotion was playacting, it didn't diminish her appreciation for what he was doing. He had worries of his own, yet he was considering her feelings and her grandfather's troubles. What a nice man he was turning out to be.

She had an impulse to run into his embrace and hug him, but she resisted, concerned that the feel of his arms about her was starting to mean too much. "Don't worry about a thing, Mr. DeMorney," she promised. "I'll be the most devoted bride you could hope for." She smiled, meaning it. "Have a good meeting."

His eyes narrowed further as she spun to go.

MERCY SPENT HER MORNING snorkeling, viewing the colorful fish that swarmed beneath the surface of Grand Cayman's warm, clear water. That noon, after stepping out of the shower, she noticed how pink her back and shoulders had gotten. Wrapping a towel about herself, she got a bottle of medicated salve out of the medical kit and perched on the edge of the bed to apply it to her stinging skin. Unfortunately she could only manage to reach her shoulders and little more. She was struggling to coat her back when the door to their suite burst open.

She was so startled, she dropped the plastic squeeze bottle on the carpet. Knowing none of the servants would barge in without knocking, she knew Damon was making a surprise visit. Whirling toward him, she protectively clutched at her flimsily tied towel. "What— why..." she squeaked, but couldn't get out more.

He was scowling. "We're going to Hell," he intoned as he shrugged out of his suit coat and began loosening his tie.

Her stomach lurched at his threat. That, coupled with the fact that he was getting undressed, unnerved her. He was stripping off his shirt now. What had happened?

Had he lost his vote and then his mind? Why was he peeling off his clothes, talking about going to hell? She clutched tighter at her towel. "Now—now, Damon," she stammered, taking a defensive backward step. "I—I can tell you're angry, and I know you've been under a strain. We both have. I also realize we both feel an attraction toward each other. But let's be rational. Animal lust won't solve anything!"

He was unbuckling his belt. With her last words, he paused, his gaze swinging to her face. "What?" he asked, his expression thunderous.

"I—I said," she began, then had to swallow several times. Her throat had gone prickly dry. "I—said, animal lust won't solve anything—not really."

He stared at her for a few tense ticks of the clock, then his expression eased. "Animal lust?" he repeated, his lips twitching. "And, my little virgin, just *who* am I supposed to be lusting after?"

She clutched tighter where her towel was fastened between her breasts. Her heart was pounding so hard she feared the violent palpitations would loosen the knot if she didn't hold it together. "Well—you came bursting in here muttering that you were going to hell. I thought—"

He drew off his belt. "Actually, I said, '*We* are going to Hell.'" He turned away to his dresser and pulled a pair of khaki shorts from a drawer. Only then did he turn back, this time amusement twinkled in his eyes. "Ms. Stewart, your virtue is safe." His lips lifted further into an actual grin. "Unless *your* animal lust gets the better of you, that is. I was irritated when I came in here. It bothers me that I've been forced to interrupt my work

because some of the wives are bored and want to go sightseeing with their husbands.''

Though he was standing there only half-dressed, there
was nothing threatening in his demeanor anymore. Confused, she asked, ''What does sightseeing have to do with
going to hell?''

''Grand Cayman has a tourist attraction by that
name.''

''Hell?''

''Unusual rock formations. Nothing so sinister as
eternal damnation.''

''I can't imagine calling any tourist attraction Hell.''

''There's a post office there. I understand it's quite the
thing to send postcards from Hell.''

''Oh?'' Mercy understood then, and smiled. ''I think
it's sweet.''

''Sweet?'' he queried crossly.

''Of course. I don't blame the wives for wanting to
sightsee with their husbands while they're here. Haven't
you ever wanted to share an experience with someone
special?''

His expression grew hostile. ''Not that I can recall.''

She had a feeling he was lying, that somewhere, deep
in his past, he was remembering closeness to someone,
and he hated the fact that he couldn't wipe the memories
from his heart. She wondered why.

''Nevertheless,'' he continued, ''this afternoon, by
majority request, we're going to Hell. It's very casual
there, so don't dress up.''

She felt stupid again and could feel her cheeks brighten
to the same fiery color as her shoulders and back. ''Yes,
sir.'' She turned away, adding, ''I'll get dressed.''

"Good Lord," he said. "You're sunburned."

She nodded, but couldn't face him as she stooped to pick up the salve. "It doesn't hurt much."

"I'll bet." She could hear his approach. "Give me that."

She looked back, confused.

He took the bottle from her fingers. "Lift your hair."

"You don't have to—"

"I know. Lift your hair."

She did as she was told, holding up her damp tresses, presenting him with her back. He began a gentle stroking below her hairline, then moved down along her spine. The cool salve felt heavenly against her stinging skin, but it wasn't only that. His tender ministrations had a melting effect on her as his fingers comforted, eased, cooled her overcooked flesh.

"You'd better wear a T-shirt from now on when you snorkel," he admonished softly.

"I will." It came out sounding like a sigh. She closed her eyes, relishing the sensations as his hands slipped below her shoulder blades and on down to the edge of her towel. His fingers halted there. "How far down are you burned?"

"I—I can reach the rest."

"It doesn't look too bad, from what I can see. But I'd better do this again tonight. Don't let me forget."

Though she offered a minimal nod, she had no intention of reminding him to touch her like that, ever again. After all, she was only human!

A few more luscious seconds passed before he finished. "I think you'll live," he said, handing her the bottle. "I'll be changed in five minutes. When you're ready, meet us in the house. I've hired some limousines for the rest of my guests, but you and I, Aunt Jo and Otis will take the Excellenta."

She experienced a surge of excitement, then squelched it. For a second she'd thought he might want them all together so that he could tell them about the audit. But, realistically, it was too soon for him to know anything. She smiled. "I can be ready in five minutes. No problem."

He nodded, rubbing the excess lotion into his hands. "I'll wait for you then." She had turned toward her dresser when he halted her with, "You really thought I was ripping off my clothes to attack you?"

She shrugged, feeling silly. Unable to look him in the eye, she admitted, "I thought maybe you'd lost the vote for control and had gone mad."

His wry chuckle filled the room. "For an innocent, Ms. Stewart, you have quite a lewd imagination. I wonder why that is?"

She knew he was tormenting her, so she decided to keep her humiliated flush to herself and refused to turn around. Instead she fished through a drawer and drew out a boxy knit crew top and matching watermelon shorts. "I'll be ready in five minutes," she mumbled.

EBANKS, AUNT JO AND OTIS were in the front seat of the Excellenta, Damon and Mercy in the back. At first, Mercy clutched her doorknob, but Damon's expression, and his wordless indication that Otis would wonder about her aloofness, made her face the fact that she needed to slide over and snuggle with her pretend husband. Reluctantly she scooted across the seat. Her expression must

have been terribly pained, because Damon grinned and
shook his head. Once he'd draped a possessive arm about
her, he leaned down, whispering, "Put your hand on my
thigh."

She jerked to stare at him. "I will not," she whispered
back. "And while we're on the subject, I don't think it's
necessary that you kiss me in public anymore. They have
the idea."

He arched a skeptical brow. "I thought you said you
were going to be the perfect bride."

She had a sinking feeling at his reminder. He was right.
She had promised. And she'd done it for a very good
reason. She tentatively cast her gaze down at his leg. He
was wearing shorts and quite a bit of his thigh was visible—solid, lightly furred and contoured with hard muscle. Swallowing, she snaked her hand out to lay it lightly
across the relatively safe area above his knee.

"There," he said, "is that so bad?"

She refused to look into his laughing eyes, but asided
under her breath, "Aunt Jo and Otis are so involved in
themselves they wouldn't notice if we were doing the
tango back here."

As if to stress Mercy's statement, Jo giggled and Otis
laughed at some private comment. She glanced at them,
her heart easing at the sound of Otis's merry laughter.
How long had it been since he'd sounded that happy? She
couldn't recall a time.

She was pulled from her contemplation when Damon
asked aloud, "What's so funny, you two?"

Jo twisted around. Mercy was chagrined to see that the
older woman's perusal immediately took in the fact that
Mercy's hand was on Damon's bare leg and Damon's

arm was draped about Mercy's shoulders. Her smile broadened. "Well, Damon," she chirped, "I love you, dearly, but I must be blunt. Our conversation is none of your business. Otis and I are old enough to have our private interests without reporting to you."

Otis turned then, grinning. His arm was about Jo's shoulders, and he patted her. Mercy thought he looked healthier. She didn't know if it was just the tan or possibly a new flush of health beneath the skin, but he looked better than she'd seen him look in years. He said, "Don't mind Josephine. She's cranky because Desi pouts when we leave. Roots under the bathroom sink and makes a bed in the clean towels. Quite a spoiled boy."

"Otis, dear, of course, you're right." Jo turned her attention to the man beside her. "I'd appreciate your opinion on how to make him behave more civilly. We must discuss it—tonight."

They tittered again and went back to their hushed chatter.

Damon bent near Mercy's ear. "Why do I feel they're having more fun than we are?"

She snapped around. "What do you mean by that?" she challenged, fearing she already knew.

He lifted his brow again in that taunting manner that was beginning to get on her nerves—or was it the feel of his rock-hard leg beneath her palm? Choosing not to dwell on it, she objected, "Don't be crude. My grandfather's in his seventies, and he's not in good health. He wouldn't be—be..."

With a vague grin, Damon looked away. His low chuckle reverberated through her body, both troubling and thrilling her.

WHEN THE EXCELLENTA pulled to a stop, the others had already poured out of their limousines and were milling around the area known as Hell. Mercy noticed that most of the little sector off the main road in West Bay was as colorful and tropical as the rest of the island. Strategically landscaped palm and sea grape trees were shrugging and ruffling in the breeze. Beyond a parking area edged with flowering shrubs, she spotted a quaint post office and several diminutive souvenir shops.

Next to them, across a strip of green grass, was a wooden boardwalk that led out over a rocky area. What lay beyond it appeared to be lush, low jungle bush. Damon entwined his fingers with hers. "Come on, darling," he prompted with a grin. "Let's join the other *loving* couples."

"You're so cynical," she retorted with a fake smile. "Why can't you just have a good time?"

"I wasn't raised to have a good time," he reminded roughly, though his expression remained charming.

They were heading toward the boardwalk. Other tourists were there, too, and the rumble of conversations was enough to drown out their strained comments. "I don't think I would have liked your grandfather," she asided, still maintaining her pleasant facade. He appeared happy, too, and though his smile didn't waver, his eyes narrowed. She had a sudden thought and asked, "What about your father? You never mention him."

Damon's grin faltered. "My father ran away to be an artist. He married an artist."

"They must have been fabulously talented. Their house is wonderful."

"Not particularly." They'd reached the boardwalk, and their steps reverberated along the wooden planks. "My grandfather gave the place to them."

Mercy was surprised to hear that. "Why would a man as hard and unfeeling as Kennard DeMorney give your parents such a palatial home? After all, didn't they abandon their family responsibilities—and most of all, didn't they abandon you?" she asked. "I don't understand why your grandfather would reward them for such despicable behavior."

Damon's eyes bored into hers. "Don't you?"

His bitter query was heavy with sarcasm. Mercy blinked and frowned, trying to sort out her thoughts, trying to make sense of the mocking challenge in his words and the dark affliction in his eyes.

"Damon! Mercy!" trilled Josephine. "You're dawdling. Come out here and have a glimpse into Hell!" She waved with one hand, but held tightly to Otis's fingers with the other. Fabricating a smile, Mercy waved back.

All at once the ugly truth of Damon's question hit her like a crippling blow. His parents had *sold* their only son to Kennard in exchange for a life of luxury in paradise. She felt sick, growing weak at the realization. It took all her strength to trudge the remaining length of the boardwalk. When she reached the end, she slumped against the railing, pulling her fingers from Damon's. For if she hadn't clutched at the rough wood with all her strength, she would have collapsed.

Someone was explaining about Grand Cayman's Hell—something about how the eerie formations resembling charred, clawing skeletons of damned souls, were really weathered rock called Ironshore. Not registering anything very clearly, she stared blankly at the grim scenery before her, thinking about damned souls and damning a few herself. Inhaling, she attempted to focus on the speaker's words, to blot out Damon's revelation.

"The Ironshore is a hard limestone," the guide was saying. "A million years ago it was pure white. Now it's been blackened by a layer of acid-secreting algae that erodes the rock into these distorted—"

She couldn't do it. She couldn't just pretend Damon had never spoken those awful words, never challenged her to understand the heartless thing that had been done to him. She spun away, covering her mouth with her hands in an effort to stifle a moan.

"Why, Mercy, honey," Jo cried, "it's not really hell. It's just an enchanting joke."

She closed her eyes, working desperately to regain her composure, but she couldn't stanch the tears. *She'd seen all the hell she could stand, today*—in Damon's eyes. He'd been an innocent little boy bartered away like a prize steer by his own mother and father!

That was no joke. It was the cruelest act of selfishness she'd ever heard of in her life.

CHAPTER NINE

MERCY SAT ON THE DOCK under a starry sky. Dangling her legs over the side, she tried to bolster her mood by inhaling the tangy sea breeze. Ten minutes ago the darkened sky had erupted into a display of fireworks off in the direction of Georgetown. She'd watched the effervescent golden bursts fill the tropical night, wondering what was going on. But her emotions were in such turmoil, she couldn't work up enough enthusiasm to go back to the house to ask.

Another golden ribbon snaked high into the sky, erupting into an expanding ball of sparkling streamers that trailed down the inky canvas, gradually disintegrating into nothingness.

Nothingness. The word stuck in her mind like a painful hook. This was Friday; the week was nearly over. The vote would be tomorrow, and after that her time with Damon would be at an end. She would have nothing left of him but her memories. How ironic. A week ago she'd hated him, but today she was in love with him, rooting for him to maintain control of his company.

She thought about Clayton Stringman. Over the past few days she'd reevaluated her opinion of him. He was far from stupid. Under that Santa Claus exterior, he was devious and self-serving. She'd overheard him reverse himself more than once while talking to different board members, telling each what they wanted to hear. What a snake! Unfortunately, from bits of conversation she'd caught in passing, he had solid support among the more fretful members of Damon's family. Nevertheless, she had a sense that Damon was running ahead.

Damon's one flaw, if you could call it that, was that he wasn't willing to exaggerate the truth or wheedle the way Clayton did. He didn't tell one cousin one thing and then turn around and say the exact opposite to another just to get votes. She was even beginning to doubt that he and Buffy had done anything lewd in his office that night she'd seen them there. Buffy had certainly kept her distance since then. Mercy found herself having the absurd notion that the woman had tried to bribe *him*, and had been rejected. Or was that just wishful thinking? She was so confused. Most especially, she was confused about why Damon hadn't told her about the audit. Surely there was news by now.

"There you are."

She turned at the sound of Damon's voice. He was nearby and she was surprised she'd been so deep in thought that she'd missed his approach. She smiled, her pulse racing.

"So you came out to enjoy the kickoff of Pirates Week?" he asked.

"Oh, that's right." She recalled now. "I'd forgotten. Don't we have to go to some sort of party tonight?"

He sat down beside her, swinging his legs over the side of the dock. The ocean splashed and roiled against the pilings, offering a sultry rhythm in the night's stillness. "A costume party. I thought you'd be changing." He indicated the latest torrent of golden glitter that lit up the night. "The fireworks display kicks off the week's festivities."

"Josephine mentioned it this afternoon. I—I guess my mind wasn't really on it." Mercy felt sadness engulf her. The last thing she wanted to do was attend another party and pretend to be a lovesick newlywed. She'd never spent so much time in her life going to so many gala parties and feeling so guilty about it.

It wasn't only the ongoing lie that upset her. The *suspense* about the audit was driving her crazy. Beyond that, she was going out of her mind waiting to hear from Otis's doctor.

She thought she'd explode if she didn't get some answers to something—*and right now.* While Damon scanned the sky, she examined his set face, his flexing jaw, his fixed eyes, and sensed he was uncomfortable with childhood memories of Pirates Week. She wanted to comfort him, to let him know that people could be caring, loving. Not all families deserted and bullied the ones they were supposed to protect and love.

Unable to hold back any longer, she touched his hand, craving closeness, wanting him to know he could trust her with his secrets.

"Damon," she whispered, "I—I know about what you're doing for Grandpa, and I think it's wonderful."

He turned to face her. "What?"

She smiled. "The *audit.* I know about the audit."

His eyes went wide for a split second, then narrowed. "How the hell did you find out?"

His sharp tone made her wince. But, naturally, a man as private as Damon would react that way—at first. "I—

I admit, I eavesdropped on the phone the night you told your lawyer to look into Otis's firing.'' She swallowed around the constriction that had formed in her throat. "It was noble of you to do that for Grandpa. The only reason I didn't mention it then was because I thought you'd want the pleasure of telling me yourself.'' She stopped, shrugged. "But you never did.'' When he said nothing, a tremor rushed through her, a premonition of sorts. "Why—why didn't you tell me, Damon?''

He gritted out a curse, turning away. His eyes were trained on the flashing fireworks, yet she had a feeling he wasn't aware of them and whatever he was seeing was very, very dark. In the tense stillness, the ocean made shushing sounds to the gossiping trade winds, as though even the elements were awaiting his answer. "Why do you think I didn't tell you?'' he finally muttered.

Shifting to come up on her knees, she said, "Because you didn't want to get our hopes up until you found something conclusive.'' She touched his hand again. It had curled into a fist. Hoping her first inclination was right, that this new dread blossoming inside her was a figment of her overwrought nerves, she ventured, "You do plan to clear Grandpa's name. That *is* it, isn't it?''

He closed his eyes. The bright flashes of the fireworks made a stark tableau of his rigid profile. "No, Ms. Stewart, that's *not* it.'' Mercy stared, frozen with fear as his nostrils flared.

He lifted his eyes to heaven and laughed aloud. The sound was so forsaken in the quiet it set the island birds aflutter in the trees. "You have a remarkably naive way of looking at the world,'' he admonished.

"What are you saying?" Her mind numbed with shock, she was unwilling to accept the awful likelihood that Damon's motives were less heroic than she'd thought. "Do you mean to say you'd cover it up if you found out Grandpa was innocent—just to keep control of your company?"

He glanced her way, his brow dipping. "I was born and bred to run Panther Automotive Corporation," he said, a lethal coldness in his tone. "The livelihood of thousands of people rests on my shoulders. I'll do what I have to do to keep everything I've built from being destroyed." He got to his feet, asking tersely, "Would you like a hand up? The dance, remember?"

Dismayed, she gaped at him. How could he be so unfeeling? Nausea rose in her throat and she felt lightheaded. "And I thought Clayton Stringman was a snake!" she cried, lurching to her feet. "He'd have to take *snake* lessons from you to be as low and slimy as you!" When she swayed unsteadily, he reached for her, but she avoided his help. "Don't touch me! And for your information, I wouldn't go anywhere with you—except to applaud at your *hanging!*"

"If it will make any difference," he said grimly, shoving his hands into his slacks pockets, "I have work to do in my office. You'll be farther away from me if you go."

Trembling, she glared at him, trying to turn her love into loathing, but she knew her unspoken pain was alive and glowing in her eyes. *Good Lord! How could she have fallen in love with this man? How could she have been so foolish and trusting?* Afraid she would fall to her knees if she didn't get somewhere to sit down, she whirled away.

"Fine," she cried. "I'll go. But if you show your face, I'm *leaving!*"

THE ROPE THAT BOUND Mercy's wrists itched. Now she understood why the tattered, eighteenth-century gown she wore was called the Captive Lady costume. When she'd joined the board members and their spouses in the house, ready to attend the costume ball, Josephine had apologized that she'd forgotten to include the piece of hemp required to bind her wrists. Then she'd proceeded to tie Mercy's hands together.

She wanted to scratch, but knew she'd spill her guava punch. Looking down at her bound hands, awkwardly clutching the cup, she shook her head. Only Aunt Jo could have come up with such an outlandish costume. Josephine had giggled, and insisted, "Naturally, you wouldn't want to dance without your darling Damon at the party." Mercy was dying inside, yearning to scream that she never wanted to see the man again, let alone dance with him! Still, since she didn't have any desire to dance with anyone else, either, she'd merely forced a smile and nodded.

Now here she was, standing in the grand ballroom of a *real* castle, surrounded by swarthy pirates, serving wenches and all manner of birds and amphibians. The whole situation seemed surreal—all these wild, otherworldly characters milling, flirting, chortling and swilling down tubs of rum punch.

Her heart constricted with sadness. Under other circumstances this would have been a once-in-a-lifetime thrill. As it was, she wanted badly to be far, far away from here, from Damon, and—though it was an impos-

sibility—to be able to forget the man she could have loved
for a lifetime.

Stifling a sneeze, she was reminded of the other piece
of the costume Josephine had neglected to include with
the dress—the powdered wig she now wore. Jo had insisted that powdered hair was all the rage in the seven-
teen hundreds. Mercy wrinkled her nose to ward off
another sneeze. Powdering one's hair may have been
what was fashionable two hundred years ago, but as far
as she was concerned, all the custom accomplished was
to make her nose tickle.

She glanced over the ballroom, looking for her grandfather and Josephine, having lost track of them in the
undulating crowd. In her search she spotted Clayton
Stringman, the biggest, beefiest hummingbird she'd ever
seen. He'd asked her to dance a couple of times, but she'd
demurred, reminding him of her tied hands. He'd seemed
inordinately interested in whether Damon was coming
tonight. She couldn't imagine his reason for asking, but
continued to insist that he would be there if he could.
Behind her bogus smile, she was praying that would *not*
happen. She didn't know if she could keep up the painful charade much longer.

She grew uneasy when she realized Clayton was still
lurking a short distance away. He was chatting with
Buffy, who looked quite in character dressed as a buxom
serving wench. Uncomfortable with the view, she swung
her glance away to inspect the room. Crystal chandeliers
threw sparkling light across the beige moiré-covered walls
and made the gilt trim glow. With the bank of paneled
doors thrown open at both ends of the long room, the

chandeliers tinkled as a blossom-scented breeze wafted over the two-hundred-odd guests.

A steel band, its members clad in flowered shirts and baggy trousers, was setting up, their break over. Mercy had tried to enjoy the music, but her thoughts had been too fragmented to distinguish between calypso, reggae and soca, though the leader announced each change in musical style for the benefit of the tourists among the throng.

She sighed, feeling drained. Placing her cup on the lavishly spread buffet table, she decided she'd search the garden area for her grandfather and Josephine, make her excuses and leave. Even knowing she'd have to brave Damon's unwelcome company on the yacht, she couldn't stand perpetrating their fraud for one more second.

Turning, she saw a red-and-green papier-mâché Pirate Parrot wearing a gray tricornered hat. She recognized the plump arms that fluttered out from beneath its stiff wings. Familiar green eyes were visible through the breathing hole in the bird's neck. "How are you, my dear?" the bird called over the general commotion. "You look pensive."

Mercy smiled without humor. "I guess I'm a little tired, Aunt Jo."

Josephine laughed. "I know your trouble." She patted Mercy's roped wrists. "You're missing Damon. It's simply a shame he works so much. To be frank, I was hoping his marriage to you would make him less driven. I suppose the years and years of Kennard's influence will take time to change. Don't fret, my child. I know he loves you."

Mercy swallowed uneasily. "Uh—where's Grandpa?"

"In the little turtle's room." Jo giggled. "Doesn't he make the cutest sea turtle you've ever seen?"

Mercy's smile was real this time, and she nodded. "If you don't mind, I think I'll go back to the yacht. You and Grandpa have a wonderful time. Just don't overdo."

"Never fear, my dear. I'm sure we—oh—" She waved off in the direction behind Mercy's head. "There's my little sea turtle now. *Yooo-hooo, Otis!*" She was already waddling away, without a second thought to their conversation. Mercy shook her head. But could she really fault Jo for being totally focused on the man she loved? Mercy had lost track of a lot of conversations during the past week, her thoughts had been so totally on Damon.

Ice spread through her stomach at the reminder of how hopelessly foolish she'd been. Anxious to escape, she turned toward the ballroom's distant entryway. The carved rosewood doors had been thrown wide to aid in circulation. Lifting her skirts as well as she could with her hands tied, she had taken only a few steps when a towering man swathed in a swirling black cloak stepped into the entrance.

The rakish buccaneer wore a black tricorne pulled low over his brow. A golden hoop hung from his left ear, and a black patch swathed one eye, giving him an ominous aura. His broad chest was glazed in blue-black silk, and his shirt was open to reveal a heavy gold chain; from it hung a hammered coin.

The lower half of his anatomy was sheathed in snug breeches that hid nothing of his masculine attributes. Self-consciously Mercy dropped her gaze to his square-cut boots. Highly polished, they rose up to hug his mighty calves before folding back at his knees in a wide cuff.

She shivered, feeling disoriented, as though she'd suddenly stepped into a dark passage of history. Somehow the bindings at her wrists made an ironic kind of sense now. She could well imagine this physically magnificent man leaping aboard some hapless sea vessel and plundering and ravishing to his heart's content.

Casting off the idiotic notion, she lifted her skirts, again intent on leaving. But when the frowning pirate glanced in her direction, she couldn't move. She just stood there, her skirts gathered up, as his one hooded eye wandered leisurely from the top of her bewigged head to her bare feet. The brooding expression on his face softened, but only slightly. Lips, wide and well formed, lifted at one corner in a way that was cynical yet compelling.

Mercy's heart pounded ferociously as the cloaked pirate began to wend his way through the throng in her direction. *No, it couldn't be,* she cried mentally. *Damon couldn't believe she'd melt into his arms tonight!* Paralyzed as she was, she could only watch as he approached. When he drew close, her gaze shot to his one silver-fringed eye, which was narrowed speculatively.

"What are you doing here?" she demanded.

"Would milady care to dance?" he asked, ignoring her accusation and holding out a hand. Though she was highly affronted, the masculine grace of his move drew her perusal. Beneath the froth of dark ruffles grazing his knuckles, she stared at his long fingers, craving their sensual touch. Hating herself for having any desire for a man who had no heart, she jerked up her bound hands. "I wouldn't dance with you *even if I could!*"

A melancholy smile trailed across his lips and he startled her by dipping low, drawing a dagger from his boot. The weapon flashed evilly, evoking from her a fearful intake of breath. With amazing adroitness, he severed the cord that bound her, then deposited the dagger out of sight. "You are free, milady," he remarked softly.

She didn't even have time to react before he turned and walked away from her. Just like that? Why that upset her, she had no idea. Certainly it was better this way. *Certainly!* Then why was she moving toward him? What did she think she was going to do? "Damon!" she called.

He stopped, turned, an inquiring expression on his face. "Yes?"

She shuffled to a halt, a flush creeping up her cheeks. "Uh—I—" Her mind was spinning. She couldn't just stand there! What was she going to say? *Don't go! I love you! Why can't you be the honorable man I thought you were?* Not if she had any sense left at all. "I wish it were that easy," she finally blurted after a couple of false starts. Tearing the remaining rope from her wrists, she cried, *"Being free of you!"* She flinched at the sob that had escaped with her words.

A look of weary sadness flashed across his features. He reached toward her, but she stumbled away. His features closing, he muttered, "I wish it were, too."

His voice had been strangely hoarse, as though he actually regretted what he had to do to save his company. Her heart took note, but she fought her upsurge of tenderness. "I hope Clayton Stringman beats you tomorrow!" she snapped back, knowing it was the most blatant lie she'd told in all her blatant lying. Lifting her skirts, she whirled away, heading for the exit, hoping she could reach the cover of darkness before her tears began to spill.

"May I have your attention, please?" someone said, and Mercy slid to a halt. She twisted around, sensing trouble. The voice was unmistakably the singsong nasal of Clayton Stringman. He'd interrupted the band and was standing on the elevated platform. Peering at Damon, she noticed that he, too, had turned, and was scowling in Clayton's direction.

The grotesque hummingbird was holding his plastic beak beneath one wing and grinning broadly at the confused crowd. "I know most of you folks don't know me. I'm Clayton Stringman, a guest here on your beautiful island, and my host is Damon DeMorney." There was a murmur in the gathering. It was clear that the locals knew of the DeMorney home, even if they'd never met the owner. Clayton indicated Damon. "There he is. And a fine host he is, too."

Most of the partygoers turned toward the handsome pirate towering over the throng, but Mercy continued to stare at Clayton, trepidation slithering along her spine. *What in the world was the man doing?* She clasped her hands together, wishing he'd get to the point.

"I've been Damon's guest for a week now," he went on, his irritating voice bouncing off every wall. "And for a week now, we've been treated to the added company of his new bride, Mercy."

To her horror, Clayton indicated where she was standing. Flushing, she lowered her eyes as several hundred strangers turned to inspect her. She hoped she didn't visibly quake under all the perplexed scrutiny.

She was sure the partygoers were as bewildered by Clayton's surprise speech as she. *Please, Clayton*, her mind railed. *Get on with it. If you're going to make one of your syrupy-sly "Notice how thoughtful and therefore worthy of the presidency I am" speeches, get it over!* This was embarrassing.

"Well, I've known Damon most of his life, and I'm fond of the boy." Mercy bit her lip. What a consummate liar the man was. "Yet, in all the years I've known him, I never realized what a jokester he could be. I thought his other guests would enjoy knowing what a trick he's played on us this week. You see, Damon is not *really* married at all. It's all been a boyish prank. I know I'm having a good laugh about it, and thought all his friends should be in on the escapade."

Mercy's head snapped up. There was a low-pitched buzzing among the members of the audience. Clearly, Damon's board members weren't taking this news in stride. Clayton's method of divulging the lie had been almost criminally deceitful, announcing it at a huge party, pretending it were a lark when in reality he was purposely ruining Damon's life in a most cruel and public way. *The slime!*

Her gaze shot to Damon. He was staring at her, his teeth clenched, his eyes communicating hard fury. It struck her then. *Damon thought she'd told Clayton about their conspiracy—to get even!*

She stood rooted there, transfixed as he stalked to her, his green gaze slashing like talons. "Congratulations," he growled. "You got your revenge with theatrical flair."

She opened her mouth to protest, to defend herself, but he cut her off. "If you think your grandfather's situation will be any better under Clayton, Ms. Stewart, you're more naive than even I gave you credit for." He glowered at her for another second, then turned away to deal with the board members converging on him. Mercy watched helplessly as he strode away, the image of a man walking into a den of hungry lions, unarmed, yet with his head held high.

Several of the board members' wives were glaring at her, but none approached. She detected condescension and disdain in their attitude and felt deep shame. She knew what they were thinking. But anything she said to try to repair her reputation would fall on deaf ears. Besides, her reputation was the least of her troubles right now.

The band began to play again, something light and lilting, but as far as Mercy was concerned it might as well be a death dirge.

Death dirge.

Her heart clenched in panic. *Grandpa!* Where was he? How had he taken the ghastly tidings? She checked over the room. Unable to see him anywhere, she prayed he'd been outside in the garden, that he hadn't heard the announcement. Rushing toward the open doors at one end of the ballroom, she prayed she'd find him out there with Josephine, so she could explain it to him, help him understand.

"Mercy! Mercy!"

She spun at the sound of Josephine's stricken voice, terror shoving her heart to her throat.

"It's *Otis*," Jo cried, struggling out of her stiff costume. Once free of it, she ignored her twisted and bunched sweat suit, waving frantically. *"He's collapsed!"*

CHAPTER TEN

MERCY HAILED Otis's doctor, a bald, penguin of a man in a white coat, scurrying down the hospital corridor. "Dr. Kayette," she called, hurrying to cut him off so that she could have a quick, private chat with him.

The doctor turned, adjusted his thick glasses, then smiled, his heavy jowls lifting in a grin when he saw who it was. "Miss Stewart," he said, his gravelly voice at odds with his diminutive, doughy stature. "You look lovely." He took both her hands in his. "I gather you've finally gotten yourself some sleep."

She squeezed his fingers fondly. "Well, once Grandpa was out of danger, I managed." She neglected to mention how a certain, silvery-haired pirate continued to invade her dreams, no matter how she tried to force him from her brain. "I just wanted to thank you, again. Grandpa's recuperating from his heart attack so well."

The doctor pursed his lips, nodding. "Extremely well, considering it's only been two weeks. I'd say much of it's due to that delightful Miss DeMorney who hovers about him." He chuckled and it sounded like a box of pebbles being shaken. "She has the demeanor of a lovable puppy, but where it comes to your grandfather, she's a tiger protecting her cub."

"Yes," Mercy agreed, abashed. She'd seen Josephine berate everyone from his day nurse to the hospital food service staff. "I—I'm sorry about that. Aunt Jo's a little one-tracked where it comes to Grandpa." She paused, swallowed nervously. "What I wanted to ask was this. You know Jo and Grandpa are getting married today. What—what would you say his prognosis is—I mean, do you think he'll..." The words trailed off. She couldn't voice her fears.

Dr. Kayette smiled kindly. "As I've said before, your grandfather had given up on life in the rest home. He was dying, and there was nothing I could do for him. When he heard about your marriage—" He stopped, shook his head, knowing it was a sore subject. "Anyway, that news gave him a will to live. And when he wanted to see you, I knew there was no stopping him. Besides," he added, pushing his glasses more securely on his beakish nose, "I couldn't refuse him what I felt would be his last chance to see you." His expression brightened. "Little did I know the effervescent Josephine DeMorney would come bubbling into his life. Between you and that little dynamo, he was starting to flourish."

"But—but the attack," Mercy reminded him.

The doctor nodded. "Ah, yes. Well, the bad news about your marriage not being real was too much for him. He was still very weak." Touching her arm reassuringly, he added, "But I believe that with his new will to live, and with plenty of rest, good nutrition and sensible exercise, he can thrive."

Mercy's eyes filled with tears of relief and gratitude. "Oh, Dr. Kayette. That's the best news I've had in— in..." She hugged his chunky shoulders, unable to go on.

"There, there," he soothed. "As I've said before, medical science can only do so much. Be grateful to yourself and that irrepressible tigress sitting in there beside him."

Mercy stepped away, wiping at a stray tear. "I—thank you, Doctor."

He pushed his glasses back again, nodding. "Well, if you'll excuse me, I have to tend to some patients who need me more than your grandfather does." He gave her a heartening grin and waddled off.

Mercy smiled tremulously, the doctor's words a balm to her bruised soul. She'd felt such guilt over the way her grandfather had found out about the marriage lie, she didn't know if she could bear it if he had died.

Shaking off the horrible thought, she looked down at her pink linen dress, smoothing out tiny wrinkles more from jangled nerves than any real need. With a despondent sigh, she wondered why she couldn't rid herself of a nagging restlessness these days.

Tucking back a strand of hair that had escaped her French twist, she reminded herself that all was well. She owed Damon a grudging debt of gratitude for having Otis airlifted to Miami, she knew. And she'd get around to writing him a polite note of thanks—someday. But right now she was too hurt. How could he have believed she was the one who'd told Clayton about the fake marriage? She'd be the last person to do anything to put her grandfather's health in jeopardy with such a negligent act.

She shook off the distressing thought and took a heartening breath. Damon was well out of her life. Grandpa was doing fine and he was happy for the first time in years. Any minute, the minister would be arriving to marry him to the woman he loved. She should be completely delirious.

She pivoted toward Otis's room, but came to a stunned halt. Unable to believe her eyes, she stared, then blinked. But the image refused to disappear.

Before her stood Damon DeMorney, a muscle throbbing in his perfect square jaw as he observed her approach.

Her breath caught in her throat, and it was painful to breathe. The man was magnificent. There was no other word to describe him. A living, breathing monument to masculinity, he wore a classic gray, custom-made suit that fit his athletic body impeccably. His shirt was snowy white and his silk tie held a subtle pattern of plum, gray and a shade of green that set off his eyes to distressing perfection.

Under the fluorescent lighting, his silver-white hair gave his face a haloed effect, making him look like some heavenly being rather than the hard-hearted businessman he was.

"What—what are you doing here?" she rasped.

His lips lifted ruefully. "It's nice to see you, too."

No matter how she tried, Mercy couldn't drag her gaze from his face. Why, oh, why, did he have to be so handsome? He was even more good-looking than in her troubling dreams, though there was a definite cast of fatigue around his eyes. She felt a jumble of emotions. Some were soft and yearning, and that irritated her. "You're not welcome here," she objected.

He crossed his arms before him. "Perhaps not by you. But I was invited to this wedding."

She blanched. Why didn't she realize Aunt Jo would never consider getting married without Damon in attendance? She only wished she'd been warned. Maybe then she could have prepared herself, feigned icy indifference.

Belatedly trying for that, she lifted her chin and breezed past him. "I won't ruin Grandpa's wedding with a quarrel. However, I don't see how you can show your face—"

There was a halting grip on her wrist. "Mercy," he cut in. "I'm sorry for thinking you told Clayton about us." She reluctantly faced him, surprised by his apology. "I know, now, he must have been the one eavesdropping on the beach that night." With undisguised contempt in his voice, he added, "It would be like him to wait for the most damaging moment to spring it on everyone."

Mercy frowned. Though she wanted badly to hate this man, her heart betrayed her by rushing to the place where his flesh touched hers. "Well—" she began breathlessly. "At—at least you've owned up to *one* of your mistakes." She inhaled and lowered her voice to mask its trembling. "I heard you got the board to put off the vote until next month. That must have taken every ounce of your gift of gab."

He shrugged. "I still have a few supporters on the board."

She eyed heaven. "You amaze me, Damon. You could talk a bull into giving milk."

Thoughtful dark eyes searched her face as he murmured, "Thank you."

"It's *not* a compliment!" Wanting the awkward contact between them to end, she jerked on his hold. "Please, let me go."

"They've found something irregular in the audit," he said, ignoring her plea. "Amos can't tell yet if it helps or hurts Otis."

She stilled. "Audit? Don't tell me you're going through with that. Why would you?"

"I guess I want to know the truth."

She gritted her teeth, her anger billowing. "Though once you find out Otis is innocent, nobody else will ever know!" She jerked again. "*Let go!* I see Reverend Gatewillow coming."

He did as she asked this time, but his fingers lingered against her wrist. It upset her that she was allowing it, that she was also delaying. With that appalling realization, she lurched toward the reverend with as much enthusiasm as she could muster, while her disobedient thoughts tarried on Damon.

JOSEPHINE WAS AS RADIANT as any bride had ever been, dressed in her Dolly Parton wig and a white silk sweat suit. She carried a bouquet of red hothouse tulips. She'd confided to Mercy that, according to her Victorian flower book, red tulips symbolized a perfect lover, which, she'd shyly admitted, her darling Otis was—and would be again once he was well.

She'd had a boutonniere made for Otis, fashioned from one red tulip and a sprig of baby's breath. He looked darling in his crisp, yellow seersucker pajamas with the bright tulip pinned over his heart. Even though he was pale, having lost his tan, he'd gained a few important pounds and looked less frail.

Josephine sat beside the hospital bed, holding his hand. The reverend had stationed himself at the foot of the bed and was reciting the marriage vows as though he were delivering a rousing sermon.

Mercy stood beside Aunt Jo, serving as her maid of honor, while Damon stood on the other side of the bed. Otis's best man.

Mercy's mind drifted from time to time, and her glance veered waywardly toward Damon. Once, he caught her looking at him and passed her a rueful grin. Disconcerted, she looked away.

Before she knew it, the reverend was pronouncing Jo and Otis man and wife. The new Mrs. Goodeve leaned over the bed and gave her husband a loving kiss on the lips, then once again on the cheek, whispering and cooing and patting his face. It was such a sweet scene, tears welled in Mercy's eyes.

Suddenly something flew at her, and in a reflex action, she reached out to defend herself. A split second later she found herself clutching Jo's bouquet. "Well, my dear," Jo said, her cheeks bright with the blush of a new bride. "I certainly hope you and Damon take the hint and get your sweet selves back together." She took Mercy's hand and reached across Otis, beckoning for Damon to grasp her fingers. "You two can deny it all you want, but I *know* you were in love back there on Grand Cayman, and legal marriage or no, you belong together!"

Mercy was mortified by Jo's declaration. She shot Damon a wide-eyed glance. He was watching her, his ex-

pression unreadable. He continued to do so even as he
bent to kiss his great-aunt's fingers. "I wish you and Otis
all the happiness in the world," he murmured, as though
he'd thought nothing of Jo's admonition at all. *Mr.
Cool. Mr. Unruffled.* When he withdrew his hand, he
transferred his gaze to Otis, squeezing the man's shoulder. "You're looking well, Grandpa."

The older man chuckled. "Thanks, my boy. But I can't
say the same for you. You seem kinda worn down. If I
was feeling a little better, I'd go give that Clay Stringman a piece of my mind for giving you such worries."

Mercy released herself from Jo's grip. "If you'll excuse me," she murmured. "I—I have to check on the
cake." It was a flimsy excuse. They all knew the cake was
across the hall in the nurses' lounge and didn't need
checking on. But she couldn't stand being near Damon
any longer. It was just too painful.

She hurried into the lounge, almost colliding with a
hospital volunteer preparing to wheel in the cake. She
told the woman to go ahead, then discovered she was still
clutching Jo's bouquet. Dropping it on the cart beside the
cake, she escaped down the hall toward the most distant
drinking fountain. She wasn't thirsty, but she decided the
long trek would serve as a delaying tactic. Surely Damon
could tell his presence upset her. If he were any kind of
gentleman he would have his piece of cake and leave.
Well, whether he realized he upset her or not, whether he
was a gentleman or not, she planned to loiter out here
until he was gone.

After a long, slow drink of water, she straightened in
time to see Damon exit her grandfather's room. He
stopped, glancing one direction, then the other. His fea-

tures grew somber when he saw her, and he plunged his hands into his slacks' pockets, watching her watch him. His stare was intense, brooding, and Mercy had the oddest sense that he was photographing her with his mind.

The strain of each ticking second that he continued to stare wore at her already abused nerves. Her lips began to quiver, and her pulse thrummed like thunder in her ears, but for some demented reason, she couldn't break eye contact.

Abruptly, his lips dipped in a deep frown and he pivoted away, his clipped tread resonating on the polished tile. When he'd disappeared around a corner, she felt a deep sense of loss, like a steel weight dropping on her heart.

MERCY WAS STARTING OVER on a brand-new yacht with a brand-new boss—and, hopefully, a brand-new lease on life. It was the first day of December, one month into Otis's recovery. Just that morning she'd seen the newlyweds off on a belated honeymoon cruise aboard the *Silver Cat*. Otis looked wonderful and was so happy. She'd wanted to go along and cook for them, but Jo confided it would be inhibiting to have her groom's granddaughter on the yacht while they were honeymooning.

She smiled to herself and shook her head, wondering what Jo and Otis had in mind that she would so inhibit them from doing. Her smile faded as she recalled Damon's amused comment back on Grand Cayman, when he'd suggested that Jo and Otis were having more fun than they were. She bit her lip, trying to sweep all thoughts of Damon from her consciousness. She had a new job on an even more luxurious yacht, with the inter-

esting name *I Love You*. The animated, pleasant captain
had gotten the opulent yacht under way a couple of hours
ago, and Mercy had just finished preparing a sumptuous
meal for two.

She hadn't met the yacht's owners—a newlywed couple—having been hired by their representative on Aunt
Jo's glowing recommendation. The man had given her
complete instructions as to the first meal—a gourmet
feast by candlelight.

The one thing she regretted about her new job was that
she would be working for a honeymooning couple. It
would be tough tamping down memories of her own
make-believe honeymoon while two young people, very
much in love, would be there to remind her during this
month-long Caribbean cruise.

When the buzzer sounded, signaling that the couple
was ready to eat, she checked her appearance in the shiny
surface of the stainless-steel refrigerator. It relieved her
to see that for once she didn't have a streak of anything
on her new white uniform.

She picked up the silver tray carrying the salads, wondering why she had such poor luck with stewardesses.
The one that was supposed to be helping with dinner had
disappeared just the way Bonnie always had on the *Silver Cat*. As she carted her burden down the hall to the
dining salon, she wondered idly if there was a stewardess
school somewhere that taught a course in Effective Dis-
appearing When It's Time To Serve Meals.

Mercy entered a salon resplendent with rich teak walls,
fine linen and gold-accented sterling. She was all smiles,
wanting to make a good first impression. But just inside
the door her smile died as dismay flew through her.

Damon DeMorney was standing there, so casually handsome in white slacks and polo shirt, it made her heart ache. He seemed his calm, collected self, his hands resting lightly on the back of one of the Queen Anne chairs.

"Hello, Mercy," he said with a small smile.

In a shocked stupor, her glance slid to the table where there were two places set. Her heart turned to ice and dropped to her feet where it shattered into a million pieces. *Had he married? Would she have to serve the man she loved on his honeymoon—with another woman? What sort of twisted vengeance was this?*

Before she knew what was happening, he'd removed the tray from her stiffened hands and set it soundlessly on the tablecloth. "It's good to see you." He took her hand. "Why don't you sit down, you look pale."

The touch of his fingers snapped her out of her paralysis, and she staggered away from his touch. "What is this?" she croaked. "Why am I here? I have no intention of working for *you!*"

"Mercy," he murmured, advancing on her and taking her gently by the shoulders. "Sit down." His eyes were compelling, his voice tender. "We have to talk."

She stiffened. "Damon, I can't think of anything you could possibly say that would—"

"I love you, Mercy," he broke in softly, but not so softly that she didn't hear the words.

She stared, disbelieving. "What—did you say?" She asked the question with a stern edge to her words, anticipating one of his tricks.

He reached up to smooth a loose strand of her hair. "I said, I love you." Indicating a chair with a nod, he asked, "Now, will you sit down?"

There was a wild fluttering in her stomach, but she refused to believe him. The man was so full of guile she didn't know what to expect anymore. Shaking her head, she backed away. He was looking at her with a seductive gleam in his eyes. She was so confused. *What in the world was his game?* "No—you don't love me. This is some sort of—of a—"

"Proposal," he murmured. Stepping forward, he gathered her into his arms and drew her against him. "Marry me."

Before she could call for help, he'd lowered his lips to hers, his kiss slow and persuasive, draining the fight from her. She found herself pressed against his lean body, relishing the male texture of him, craving more.

He wrapped his arms more securely about her, his hands delighting the hollow of her back, quickly drawing from her the last shreds of her resistance. She moaned, her brain battling with her emotions—her need at war with her good sense. Had he really proposed marriage? Had he meant it? And even if he had, could she marry a man with so few scruples? For a heartbeat she swayed between sweet temptation and painful truth, that knife-thin edge encountered by all lovers.

Issuing up all her disgust of his amoral business methods, she fought her desire, wrenching her lips from the wonder of his. "You have a colossal ego, Damon," she panted, promising herself that she wouldn't fall prey to his infamous empty promises. "Now, let me go before I scream for help!"

"Who do you think will come to your aid?" he countered, his tone husky and disconcertingly intimate. "This is my yacht."

She shivered at the thought. He was right. She was at his mercy. Feeling miserable, she could only stare into his eyes, so near, so alluring. Why did she have to love him? Why did her body have to quiver for his touch? She could never give herself to a man she didn't respect. "I—I think maybe I'd better sit down," she managed at last.

He led her to a chair, then took a seat beside her. When his thigh brushed hers, she tried to move away, but found she was too weak even for that.

He chuckled. For the first time since she'd known him, his laughter was devoid of cynicism. "Your lie about being married to me was a stroke of luck," he said. "It got me to initiate that audit."

She shifted to focus on his face. He was looking at her with a tenderness she'd never seen before. And he seemed in a strangely good mood. Of course, he wasn't the one being held captive on a ship at sea!

"It was another stroke of luck that day in the hospital after you left Otis's room," Damon went on, "when your grandfather reminisced about working for the company, about Clayton's father, Seymour, the original bookkeeper. The remark about Seymour being a genius with figures, was what got me thinking."

Mercy frowned, trying to follow what he was saying, but his scent clung to her, taunted her with every breath she inhaled, making it hard for her to concentrate. "Thinking?" she echoed.

He nodded. "About how a genius bookkeeper might be able to frame someone else for embezzlement."

Mercy stared at him, uncomprehending. She tried to shake the cobwebs of longing from her brain. His nearness had become so debilitating, she couldn't even trust her hearing anymore. It was all garbled and sounded so far away. But it seemed as though he was telling her that someone named Seymour had been the real embezzler all those years ago.

Damon grinned. "I was afraid, for a while, it had been my grandfather." He shook his head, his smile fading slightly. "It's not as though Kennard was an angel by any stretch of the imagination, but I needed to know if he was a thief, too."

Mercy sat up, stunned. *That was what he was saying!* Seymour Stringman had embezzled from the company, and then framed Otis for the crime.

"Of course, Seymour's dead," he explained. "But finding out about him got me curious about something else. That's when I ordered the confidential company audit. The report that came back yesterday."

She stared blankly at him. "Yesterday," she repeated, at a loss as to what he was talking about now.

"The irregularities uncovered in Clayton's department went back years. Kickbacks, out-and-out thievery. Obviously Seymour passed along his genius with fixing numbers to his son."

Mercy's lips dropped open when she understood what he was saying. Clayton Stringman was not only a conniving sneak, but he was a swindler, too! She'd always blamed the DeMorneys—hated them—and all the time they'd been as innocent of wrongdoing as her grandfather!

"So," he went on, "as of today, I'm undisputed president of Panther Automotive Corporation and Clayton is facing fraud charges. The story should be making newspaper headlines about now."

"Oh, Damon..." she breathed, his revelations finally piercing her benumbed brain. But her happiness was tainted. Otis was *innocent*, yet he hadn't even mentioned that. Apparently that was insignificant as far as he was concerned. "Of course, I—I'm happy for you, but that doesn't change—" Finding strength in her feelings of injustice to her grandfather, she vaulted up and moved away from his dangerous nearness. She couldn't forgive him for not publicly clearing his name. It was so little to ask, after all! "I insist that you turn this boat around and take me back," she blurted, heading toward the exit.

When he made no protest, she found herself slowing. *The man had proposed marriage to her!* How many times had she had that dream, only to awaken and find it disappear like a flimsy mist. Why had he done it? He couldn't *really* love her and treat her grandfather so heartlessly. To her, that was an unforgivable sin.

At the door she found herself going stock-still. Unable to help herself, she twisted around. "You have everything you want now," she accused, her voice ragged. "I hope it makes you happy...."

"I have everything—but you," he admitted, his gaze dark and earnest.

She felt stricken, torn, but knew she could never be content with a man so selfish and cold as Damon had been raised to be. "I couldn't love a man who would treat my grandfather with such indifference."

He seemed mystified, and gave her a searching look. "I was never indifferent, Mercy. But in my own defense, I didn't know until yesterday whether I'd even have a company. After I was sure I did, I offered Otis half my stock. But you know that. You know he turned me down, said we'd work something out that was fair."

"You—you're a liar," she stormed. "I don't know any such thing!"

She saw doubt flicker in his eyes. "I'm sorry. I honestly thought he'd told you." He ran a distracted hand through his hair. "Maybe he didn't say anything because I also said I loved you and I was going to ask you to marry me today." His lips lifted in a melancholy smile. "Possibly he thought I'd want to tell you, myself. He wouldn't be the first person in your family to make that mistake."

Something Otis said this morning came rushing back to her. He'd winked, remarking cryptically, "Jo and I have a surprise for you, Messy Miss. But not here or now. If I don't miss my guess, it will find you." She'd been confused, but promptly forgotten it in her happiness for them. Could Grandpa have meant *this?*

Brooding, tender eyes ranged over her face. "Forgive me, Mercy. I guess—" He broke off, his voice rough with emotion. Clenching his jaw, he got himself under control. "I guess I went about this backward. But the minute I saw you, I just wanted to hold you and love you."

Her breathing became shallow and painful, her whole body trembling. So much was happening so fast, she couldn't think. With a perplexed shake of her head, she cried, "It can't be..."

He wiped one hand wearily across his face. "There's been a lot of lying in our relationship, but this isn't one of them." Closing the distance between them, he took her face between his hands. "Mercy, my grandfather made mistakes, my parents made mistakes, and so have I. I've had a twisted idea about love, marriage and family. But seeing you with your grandfather, watching you go to impossible lengths to help him, experiencing your loyalty through him—all that has shown me that it doesn't have to be the way it was with my family."

There was a bleak, unhappy beauty in his features that touched Mercy somewhere she'd never been touched before. He was finally showing her an inner vulnerability that had been buried with his lost childhood, and the sight thrilled her to the depths of her soul. "I do love you, Mercy," he promised softly. "If you'll give me a chance, I'll prove it to you—for the rest of our lives."

His fingers were warm and gentle against her face, his gaze hypnotic and loving. The passion she saw glimmering in his emerald eyes beckoned irresistibly. "You brought innocence and loyalty into my life, and I don't want to lose you. I love you and your messes—even your lies—for they're selfless lies meant to ease pain." He lowered his face to kiss first one eyelid and then the other. "I ask you again, Mercy. Marry me."

Her thoughts spun and skidded, her senses reeled. "I don't believe you're lying." She sighed, her heart racing with joy. "I don't believe you are."

With a bewitching flash of teeth, he lifted her into his arms. "Oh, you don't?" he queried, a teasing note coming into his voice. "What's the name of this yacht, Mercy?"

Confused, she murmured, *"I Love You."*

His chuckle was rich and deep, and she sensed that he was once again whole. "I love you, too, darling," he vowed. "And I'll take that as a yes. Luckily my captain is also a minister."

She looked dreamily into his face, at last allowing herself to accept the enchanting reality that he loved her. She smiled back. "That *is* lucky."

"To be honest, luck had nothing to do with it," he confessed, nibbling at her earlobe. "I interviewed all night. Flew this guy in from California this morning."

A laugh gurgled in her throat. "You should be in bed."

"Suddenly that idea has a certain appeal," he whispered. "Now, kiss me."

She did as commanded, and his lips parted hers in a soul-searing message of undying devotion.

That evening, after a brief wedding ceremony, Damon and Mercy began their married life together—no longer make-believe, and utterly devoid of lies. They were lovers destined to be only slightly less contented in the galley, creating gourmet feasts for the palate, than in their marriage bed, creating passionate feasts for the soul.

RUGGED. SEXY. HEROIC.

OUTLAWS *and* HEROES

Stony Carlton—A lone wolf determined never to be tied down.

Gabriel Taylor—Accused and found guilty by small-town gossip.

Clay Barker—At Revenge Unlimited, he *is* the law.

JOAN JOHNSTON, DALLAS SCHULZE and MALLORY RUSH, three of romance fiction's biggest names, have created three unforgettable men—modern heroes who have the courage to fight for what is right....

OUTLAWS AND HEROES—available in September wherever Harlequin books are sold.

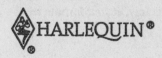

OUTH

Bestselling Author

Introduces you to the woman called

Everybody loves Red—whoever she is. A haunted
teenager who defied the odds to find fame as a top model.
A pretty face who became a talented fashion photographer.
A woman who has won the love of two men. Yet, no
matter how often she transforms herself, the pain of Red's
past just won't go away—until she faces it head on....

Available this July, at your favorite retail outlet.

MIRA The brightest star in women's fiction   MESR

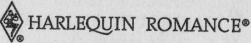

HARLEQUIN ROMANCE®

brings you

A letter has played an important role in all our romances in our Sealed with a Kiss series so far, but next month's THE BEST FOR LAST by Stephanie Howard is a story with a difference—

All her adult life Cassandra Redmund had kept a diary. It had detailed the disastrous ending to her relationship with Damon Grey years before and, now, her present predicament.

She had run into him again on a Caribbean island paradise only to discover that Damon's charm was as persuasive as ever—and just as dangerous. She was determined she wouldn't give in...but was Cassandra's fate about to be sealed with a kiss?

Available wherever Harlequin books are sold.

SWAK-6

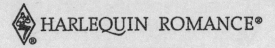

HARLEQUIN ROMANCE®

brings you

Romances that take the family to heart!

A FAMILY CLOSENESS by Emma Richmond

If Davina's fiancé hadn't run off with her best friend, she wouldn't have got involved with Joel Gilman. And now, four years after their disastrous encounter, it seemed that time hadn't dulled their mutual attraction! But Joel had a new woman in his life now—his young daughter, Ammy. And when he asked her to look after the little girl, Davina had a temporary chance to experience what might have been—and what she'd always wanted....

Coming next month, from the bestselling author of
MORE THAN A DREAM!

FT-3

THREE BESTSELLING AUTHORS

HEATHER GRAHAM POZZESSERE
THERESA MICHAELS
MERLINE LOVELACE

bring you

THREE HEROES THAT DREAMS ARE MADE OF!

The Highwayman—He knew the honorable thing was to send his captive home, but how could he let the beautiful Lady Kate return to the arms of another man?

The Warrior—Raised to protect his tribe, the fierce Apache warrior had little room in his heart until the gentle Angie showed him the power and strength of love.

The Knight—His years as a mercenary had taught him many skills, but would winning the hand of a spirited young widow prove to be his greatest challenge?

Don't miss these **UNFORGETTABLE RENEGADES!**

Available in August wherever Harlequin books are sold.

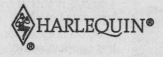HARLEQUIN®

HREN

FLYAWAY VACATION SWEEPSTAKES!

This month's destination:

Glamorous LAS VEGAS!

Are you the lucky person who will win a free trip to Las Vegas? Think how much fun it would be to visit world-famous casinos... to see star-studded shows...to enjoy round-the-clock action in the city that never sleeps!

The facing page contains two Official Entry Coupons, as does each of the other books you received this shipment. Complete and return all the entry coupons— **the more times you enter, the better your chances of winning!**

Then keep your fingers crossed, because you'll find out by August 15, 1995 if you're the winner! If you are, here's what you'll get:

- Round-trip airfare for two to exciting Las Vegas!
- 4 days/3 nights at a fabulous first-class hotel!
- $500.00 pocket money for meals and entertainment!

Remember: The more times you enter, the better your chances of winning!*

*NO PURCHASE OR OBLIGATION TO CONTINUE BEING A SUBSCRIBER NECESSARY TO ENTER. SEE REVERSE SIDE OF ANY ENTRY COUPON FOR ALTERNATIVE MEANS OF ENTRY.

VLV KAL

FLYAWAY VACATION
SWEEPSTAKES
OFFICIAL ENTRY COUPON

This entry must be received by: JULY 30, 1995
This month's winner will be notified by: AUGUST 15, 1995
Trip must be taken between: SEPTEMBER 30, 1995-SEPTEMBER 30, 1996

YES, I want to win a vacation for two in Las Vegas. I understand the prize includes round-trip airfare, first-class hotel and $500.00 spending money. Please let me know if I'm the winner!

Name_____

Address _____ Apt. _____

City   State/Prov.   Zip/Postal Code

Account #_____

Return entry with invoice in reply envelope.

© 1995 HARLEQUIN ENTERPRISES LTD.   CLV KAL

FLYAWAY VACATION
SWEEPSTAKES
OFFICIAL ENTRY COUPON

This entry must be received by: JULY 30, 1995
This month's winner will be notified by: AUGUST 15, 1995
Trip must be taken between: SEPTEMBER 30, 1995-SEPTEMBER 30, 1996

YES, I want to win a vacation for two in Las Vegas. I understand the prize includes round-trip airfare, first-class hotel and $500.00 spending money. Please let me know if I'm the winner!

Name_____

Address _____ Apt. _____

City   State/Prov.   Zip/Postal Code

Account #_____

Return entry with invoice in reply envelope.

© 1995 HARLEQUIN ENTERPRISES LTD.   CLV KAL

OFFICIAL RULES

FLYAWAY VACATION SWEEPSTAKES 3449

NO PURCHASE OR OBLIGATION NECESSARY

Three Harlequin Reader Service 1995 shipments will contain respectively, coupons for entry into three different prize drawings, one for a trip for two to San Francisco, another for a trip for two to Las Vegas and the third for a trip for two to Orlando, Florida. To enter any drawing using an Entry Coupon, simply complete and mail according to directions.

There is no obligation to continue using the Reader Service to enter and be eligible for any prize drawing. You may also enter any drawing by hand printing the words "Flyaway Vacation," your name and address on a 3"x5" card and the destination of the prize you wish that entry to be considered for (i.e., San Francisco trip, Las Vegas trip or Orlando trip). Send your 3"x5" entries via first-class mail (limit: one entry per envelope) to: Flyaway Vacation Sweepstakes 3449, c/o Prize Destination you wish that entry to be considered for, P.O. Box 1315, Buffalo, NY 14269-1315, USA or P.O. Box 610, Fort Erie, Ontario L2A 5X3, Canada.

To be eligible for the San Francisco trip, entries must be received by 5/30/95; for the Las Vegas trip, 7/30/95; and for the Orlando trip, 9/30/95.

Winners will be determined in random drawings conducted under the supervision of D.L. Blair, Inc., an independent judging organization whose decisions are final, from among all eligible entries received for that drawing. San Francisco trip prize includes round-trip airfare for two, 4-day/3-night weekend accommodations at a first-class hotel, and $500 in cash (trip must be taken between 7/30/95—7/30/96, approximate prize value—$3,500); Las Vegas trip includes round-trip airfare for two, 4-day/3-night weekend accommodations at a first-class hotel, and $500 in cash (trip must be taken between 9/30/95—9/30/96, approximate prize value—$3,500); Orlando trip includes round-trip airfare for two, 4-day/3-night weekend accommodations at a first-class hotel, and $500 in cash (trip must be taken between 11/30/95—11/30/96, approximate prize value—$3,500). All travelers must sign and return a Release of Liability prior to travel. Hotel accommodations and flights are subject to accommodation and schedule availability. Sweepstakes open to residents of the U.S. (except Puerto Rico) and Canada, 18 years of age or older. Employees and immediate family members of Harlequin Enterprises, Ltd., D.L. Blair, Inc., their affiliates, subsidiaries and all other agencies, entities and persons connected with the use, marketing or conduct of this sweepstakes are not eligible. Odds of winning a prize are dependent upon the number of eligible entries received for that drawing. Prize drawing and winner notification for each drawing will occur no later than 15 days after deadline for entry eligibility for that drawing. Limit: one prize to an individual, family or organization. All applicable laws and regulations apply. Sweepstakes offer void wherever prohibited by law. Any litigation within the province of Quebec respecting the conduct and awarding of the prizes in this sweepstakes must be submitted to the Regies des loteries et Courses du Quebec. In order to win a prize, residents of Canada will be required to correctly answer a time-limited arithmetical skill-testing question. Value of prizes are in U.S. currency.

Winners will be obligated to sign and return an Affidavit of Eligibility within 30 days of notification. In the event of noncompliance within this time period, prize may not be awarded. If any prize or prize notification is returned as undeliverable, that prize will not be awarded. By acceptance of a prize, winner consents to use of his/her name, photograph or other likeness for purposes of advertising, trade and promotion on behalf of Harlequin Enterprises, Ltd., without further compensation, unless prohibited by law.

For the names of prizewinners (available after 12/31/95), send a self-addressed, stamped envelope to: Flyaway Vacation Sweepstakes 3449 Winners, P.O. Box 4200, Blair, NE 68009.

RVC KAL